Mended

Book 4

Of the Abigail fate series

By

Adele Lea

Dedicated to the memory of our
two special Angels.
Never forgotten, and always in
our hearts.
Mummy & Daddy

xx

As Abigail's journey unfolds through the chapters of her life, it becomes real and you feel a sense of her heartache, her sadness, and pain.
You're willing her, as you turn the pages, to succeed in chasing her dreams and to finally free herself from Adam.

But nobody said life was easy.
So, the moral to this tale, my friends, is: "Never give up on your dreams, chase them as far as you can, because one day you may catch them and have your, happy-ever-after."

For George, my son - the reason I breathe.

Thank you for reading,

Adele -x-

Chapter 1

I've stood so many times like this before just staring into space, as a child, as an adult, trying to remember nice thoughts, nice memories, but the more I stood trying to remember, the more I forgot. All I could ever remember were the negatives. Maybe that's all I had to remember. The past years have certainly been negative, nothing nice sprang to mind. I sometimes think you see what you want to see, instead of seeing what is actually there, what is true, or what really matters.

And yes, I'm staring again through the window, however today I've no negative thoughts or memories, because my mind is filled with new memories, fresh memories, memories that I'm making with Edward.

I'm remembering us standing in this exact spot. His arms were tight around my waist, my head resting against him, and I can recall exactly what was said by him and what was said by me.

"Well, have we to go and get a tree for in here?" He laughed loudly, as I almost squealed my reply.

"Oh, yes. Our first Christmas together!"

"Go and get your boots on then while I get the spade."

"The spade!" I shouted, as he darted through the door like an over excited child.

I smile seeing us in my mind dragging the tree up the garden, Shadow prancing around barking, thinking it was some fantastic game. Afterwards, we showered, then sat for hours, eating Chinese food on the rug in front of the open fire admiring our handy-work and we agreed, 'Next Christmas we'd buy one.' We then sat a little stunned with each other knowing that unconsciously we'd made a commitment, by saying, 'Next Christmas.' But it felt right, that it was meant-to-be. Edward I wasn't sure about, I think he meant it, although I don't want to read too much into it, well not for now anyway. I'm just enjoying this time with him, getting to know him and savouring my happy memories, because for once, it feels nice to have these thoughts to remember.

A warm feeling grows inside recalling how bossy he is. He nags if I don't eat, nags if I exercise too much, and worries when I'm out too long running with Shadow. I've also learnt how competitive he really is - especially when I told him, I thought, 'he'd an ulterior motive for not wanting me to exercise, and that he was really worried because he knew I'd whip his arse, especially now that I was feeling a hundred-per-cent better.' To be fair I knew I'd never be able to whip his arse, but I wasn't about to admit that to him. I watch him in the mornings from the window in the bedroom, running on the path towards the beach, and boy is he fast. I think Shadow had a hard time keeping up with him. I honestly don't know where he gets his stamina from. A shiver of tingles runs down my spine knowing he's proven his promise to me morning, noon and night, although to be honest, I don't mind that promise in the slightest. I think we've christened every single room, including the barn and garage, another warm tingle flushes over me as I remember the Aston Martin - wow that was a long exhilarating afternoon. The only place we've not christened is the downstairs cloakroom, which I commented on, and he laughed raising an eyebrow as if to say, 'It was early days.' Then chased me around the house until he caught me, and like the Neanderthal he is, carried me over his shoulder to the bedroom and had his wicked way with me, again. And, yes, of course my resistance was feeble. I loved it just as much as him. The baubles jingle on the Christmas tree behind me, like wind chimes ringing in a slight breeze. I turn seeing Shadow walking past, his large bushy tail brushing against the needles and releasing the sweet scent of pine into the air. The tree sways gently and the fairy-lights chase each other leisurely around the branches. It's magical and hypnotic to watch. As my eyes follow the lights down towards the base, my smile widens, although I'm not certain it could get any wider, but it does, as I see all the presents underneath the tree which are mainly for me from Edward. He does spoil me far too much. I've placed his Christmas card behind his main present, the Rolex I bought from Forbes which I had engraved. Engraved with words that I've not spoken to him, but every single one of them I mean. I just hope that he likes it and the card. The present is sort of in two parts. I need him to read the card before he opens his present. I sat yesterday on the rug in front of the fire writing the words on a piece of paper, then reading them back to Shadow, who was my audience. When I was happy, I sat at the table in the kitchen writing them in the beautiful card I've chosen. I know Edward won't get the significance of it and probably won't understand what it means to me. That's because I've never told him about my dreams, but it made me feel happy when I saw it- it reminded me so much of the beautiful dream I had. My happy-ever-after. The card is handmade with no message or words inside with a picture on the front that had caught my eye a Robin sitting proudly on a snowy white tree which instantly reminded me of the Robin in my dream, and what a nice dream that was. I remember thinking at the time, 'I wish my life was like that dream' and now I can say it is. I've no little boy, but I've got Edward and Shadow. Shadow plonks himself against my leg breaking my train of thought as he pushes his head against me nudging me to stroke him, but his eyes don't stop looking in front as he's waiting with patience for his master to return. I pull in a deep breath, thinking It's Christmas Eve already, as I watch the snow fall, gently fluttering past the window and I can almost see the patterns of the snowflakes; they remind me of sparkling glitter doilies falling gracefully onto the sill. I pat Shadow, "Hey, have you come to wait for Edward too?" His head cocks to one side because I've spoken Edwards name, his eyes bright and alert. He's so clever, I think, rewarding him with a rub behind his ear, so he presses against my leg.

"Christmas Eve, Shadow. I can't wait for tomorrow I'm so excited." He stares, so I pull a daft face, continuing to speak as though he's listening to every word I'm saying.

"You're a very good listener boy, have you ever thought of going into counselling?" I laugh loudly, rolling my eyes, well-aware that I'm having a one-sided conversation with the dog. As I bend facing him placing my hand at the top of his head then I rag him, he gets excited and stands, his wide bushy tail wagging, his eyes fixed on me excited and he's waiting for what's coming next,

"Go!" I shout, he barks, then turns and runs from the room skidding on the polished wood floor as I chase him. He runs down the hallway before bounding up the steps looking behind to see if I'm still there. I love this game we play together. He halts at the turn and crouches his head forward, bum in the air, tail wagging, as if he's about to pounce. I giggle - he barks, and I run up the steps to get him. This is how our game of chase always begins. Shadow crouching until I'm a quarter of the way up, and as always, he bolts off and hides in one of the bedrooms waiting for me to find him. But as I'm making my way up towards him, his ears prick up, and he starts running down past me. I make a grab for his collar, but he's too fast, making his way to the front door barking.

"Oh…is Edward here? Is that why you don't want to play with me anymore." He barks again staring at the door. I grin, thinking, I was right making my way down the rest of the steps. He's very keen to get out to him, pushing me, nudging me, and almost telling me to open the door.

"Gosh you're very excited." I say, turning the key. But there's no car on the drive, the gates are still locked. He flies past me sniffing the air and running down the drive. "Shadow come back." I shout, but he ignores me and continues running towards the gates. He bolts abruptly sniffing the ground then turns making his way back towards the house.

"Come on." He moves left towards the garage and stable block. I tut as he ignores me again.

I turn quickly heading towards the cloak room, grabbing a coat, and pulling on my boots before running back outside. "Shadow come-on-boy." He's out of sight. I try whistling, but I'm not very good. So, I continue to shout, although I hear him barking and snarling at the horses. "Oh hell." I gasp running toward the stable block, knowing if he's in with the horses he'll get trampled if he spooks them. I'm panicking and he's still snarling, the horses are whinnying. As I approach closer, I notice the door at the side of the barn is open and banging against the wall. I'm a little scared as I enter, it's dark inside and eerie. I've not been in here, well not on my own before. The horses are pacing in their individual stalls because something has spooked them. "Shush, it okay," I whisper trying to calm them but really trying to calm myself. "Shadow, where are you?" I call in a low tone, the sensor light dimly glows and I'm able to see a little better, but I can't see him or hear him, he's gone. I run back outside just to see him turning at the side of the house heading towards the vegetable patches. It's still snowing and now dark, the grounds slippery as I turn quickly around the side of the house trying my best to catch him up. I slip on some ice and try to stop myself from falling, but I can't, and I fall hard hitting the ground instinctively put my hands down to stop my head from banging on the hard path. I shout him again, looking towards the vegetable patches and cursing him knowing he's probably chasing a rabbit, suddenly I hear three loud whistles, then footsteps crunching on the gravel approaching around the corner as I turn my head and look up to see Edward standing there, his eyebrows raise in puzzlement to see me on the floor, but I'm annoyed with the dog, so I snap my greeting.

"You need a bloody babysitter for that dog of yours."

Edward merely stares not knowing what the situation is with his hand held out. I take it begrudgingly and start to stand but continue my rant.

"Don't even ask." He whistles again, before moving slightly forward. A security light comes on and I can now see Shadow sniffing the ground, his head lifts and turns towards Edwards but not before I notice fresh footprints in the snow.

"Edward has someone been here in the garden - tonight I mean - was it Jimmy - is that what Shadow heard in the garden - was it Jimmy that made him run out like he did?" I ask still looking at the footprints.

He doesn't answer but looks on towards the vegetable patches then a little further towards the gates that lead through onto the grassed area towards the beach. His eyes return to me. He smiles weakly, then nods. I think he looks puzzled.

"Was it Jimmy?"

"Yes, it was Jimmy." His reply is firm, and he continues looking towards Shadow then back at me.

"Well, is he still here? because I think you need to tell him to remember to bolt the doors next time to the stable block before he leaves. And you could have told me he was here, then I'd have known, and at least I'd have not let Shadow out. God, anything could have happened to him in there with the horses and I thought it was you on the drive, because Shadow was making such a song and dance to get out to you. So, I let him out, but he bolted towards the gates like he did before then towards the stable block. I could hear the horses and Shadow snarling at the them. I was so scared he was going to get hurt because he'd spooked them, or even get trampled." I huff getting annoyed as my arse is stinging, and he's not even bothered to ask if I'm okay. He seems more bothered about looking around the grounds. "I'm going inside my arse is wet and stinging but thanks for asking if I'm okay. And don't forget to lock the stable and get your bloody dog under control." I ramble starting to walk away.

"Hey," he snaps, grabbing for my hand. "Take a breath."

I sigh, knowing I did go on and on, but hell anything could have happened, and I think he would have been more cross at me if it had.

I roll my eyes but continue, "Can't you see the implications of what could have happened?"

"Yes, of course I can, but he's not hurt, and the horses are fine."

"Umm... thanks to me." I mutter under my breath but loud enough for him to hear.

"Yes, Abbie, thanks to you." He answers, but the words he's just spoken appear flat as though he's giving me an answer to a different question and telling me to shut up.

I get the message quickly, rolling my eyes again knowing there's no point in me continuing when he's in this mood.

I look towards Shadow, he's wet through from the snow just sat staring at Edward, as he pat's his head.

"Okay, Boy?" I raise my eyes, cross at the situation. "And you Abbie, are you okay?"

"Yes. I suppose so." I quip but really, I want to stick my tongue out at them both and I'm aware that's childish and of course if I do, he'll remind me of that fact. He pulls a sad face, so I turn my head and stare at the dog who is now giving me the puppy dog eyes. I think, as I stare at them both in turn. *'I can't even win a bloody argument with the dog.'* But deep down I know I can't be cross with either of them. I suppose Shadow was just doing his job, and Edward well he didn't know what was going on. He smiles, and when he smiles at me, well it makes me forgive him almost anything. He squeezes my hand as though to say, am I forgiven. So, I squeeze it back letting him know he is. Shadows tail wags as he walks at Edwards side, and we continue towards the house.

"I'll just lock the stable, Abbie. You go inside with Shadow. Shadow go with Abbie." The dog stares at Edward, he bends towards him. "Guard." I think he's just whispered as he now makes his way over to me.

"Edward, did you just tell Shadow to guard me, what's going on?"

He look's surprised, "did I heck as like." But I'm not at all sure I believe him.

"Are you sure." His eyes narrow as if he thinks I don't believe him.

"Yes. I'm sure Abbie, now please go inside, and change out of those wet clothes… Aren't you supposed to be surprising your Gran at the carol service." He adds as frosty as the snow on the ground.

I nod, although I'm still not convinced. I know I'm a lot of things, but deaf I'm not, but I let it ride, because I'm not sure what he said, and I'm well-aware I've to change.

I start walking in and up the stairs. Shadows hot on my heels. I shake my head a little confused, but manage a smile, thinking about my Gran and knowing how happy and pleased she's going to be.

Four years she's secretly waited for this. Every year she'd ask me if I was going to the service and every year, I'd make up a lame excuse as to why I couldn't go. She never quizzed me, or pried, but smiled softly with such a genuine smile of love and affection which broke my heart each-and-every time, because I knew I couldn't tell her the reason. I've missed so much of my life and my Grans life because of Adam, always to scared, to worried, or to brainwashed to fight back. I pat Shadow on the head whilst entering the bedroom and whisper,

"But not this year Shadow." And as normal he cocks his head to one side, which always reminds me of Edward. I pull in a deep breath, then release it with warm affection, shaking my head at my new self, "but not this year, eh, Shadow." I say again. He barks this time as though he's agreeing with what I'm saying.

I'm changed into dry clothes and start making my way from the bedroom excited about seeing Gran. I can't wait to see her face. It will be like when I was a little girl again. Carols by Candlelight.

Chapter 2

I'm in the hallway waiting for Edward, he's just finishing a call I think, as he's just replied, "Okay." He turns placing his phone into his trouser pocket. "I'm sorry...That was the hospital on the phone they need me to go in. I'm not going to be able to make the Carol service."

"Really."

"Sorry."

I smile weakly knowing how much I wanted him to come. I'm so disheartened, but I don't say, because I know how important his job is. Although I think he can see the disappointment written all over my face, he reads me so well. His eyes raise, his voice is silly, but firm. "Doctor Kildare strikes again." I grin, knowing he's trying his best to make light of the situation.

"Umm... but you're my Doctor Kildare, and you're going to have to make it up to me." I wink, and he knows he's forgiven.

"Anything in mind." He asks with a wicked grin on his face, the one he knows I can't resist.

"Umm, Yes, I'm sure I can think of something."

He nods, "Don't you worry your sweet little head about details, leave that up to me." That wicked grin has now turned dark sending tingles down my spine. As I know exactly what he's thinking now. He smiles knowing how easy I am. "Come Abbie, let's get you to church." I nod making my way inside the car. "I'll drop you off then drive onto the hospital."

As I stand alone outside the church before making my way up the path that leads to the entrance, I inwardly smile entering the porch and in through the large Oak door. The lights are bright as people make their way to their pews. The nativity is set to the side at the back, I glance at it affectionately remembering getting all excited- on Christmas eve with Gran and Glenda. I've to suddenly step back as a group of small excitable children rush past making their way to the little door that leads to the balcony in the eves. Their hymn sheets rustling in their hands as they chatter to each other nervously and the choir master mutters, 'shush,' it's all getting very exciting, the brass band on the alter steps are tuning up their instruments and a que has formed for the candles. Nostalgic, that's what this is - A country Church with its congregation and traditions. Traditions I've let laps. The smell of the fresh holly, pinecones and winter garlands catch my nostrils as I scan the Church quickly looking for Gran, then spot her next to Glenda. She's talking to someone in the isle, her backs towards me as I slowly make my way down to her. Glenda turns seeing me. I shake my head placing my finger to my lips and she nods with a smile understanding as I slide my hands around my Grans waist from behind. She suddenly tenses, then as I speak, I feel her relax. "Room for a little one on your pew." She turns quickly with the biggest smile on her face, before pulling me into a warm embrace.

"Always room on my pew for a little one." Her voice is laced with such emotion it makes me want to cry with joy. Glenda smiles, speaking eagerly.

Turning on the fairy lights inside checking the bulbs and switching the lights on to the trees outside. They both loved doing it. I smile knowing what William will be doing now. They had their routine tuned to a fine art. I can almost hear Grandad saying,

'William, mince pie time, start the ovens. Pans on for the mulled wine, it's cold outside they'll all want a warm drink.'

'I that's true George, but let's have a little tipple first before the wives arrive.' They'd laugh as though they were being naughty by having a hot toddy before Gran and Glenda caught them. They'd walk around the deli, then check outside, making the final preparations to the grotto. Then when they were both satisfied with their handywork, Grandad would go inside and get ready for his grand- finale as Father Christmas. William would head of to the kitchens on mince pie and mulled wine duty. They ran the event like a well-oiled engine. Every year it was a roaring success and any money's that were made always went to the children's home with a very generous donation from Gran and Grandad. I breathe in a secret smile for Grandad. Then one for William knowing it must hurt him doing it alone now, but it's nice of him to step in.

Every year they'd take the grotto from the basement at the deli, painting it, while Gran and Glenda wrapped the presents for the children. I used to put the labels on that read, 'Merry Christmas, from Santa.' I have to say though it somewhat confused me as a small child as to why Gran and Glenda wrapped the presents, and I stuck the labels on them, and why Santa's little helpers didn't do it. Gran told me when I'd asked one year.

"That we were in fact Santa's little helpers."

I was puzzled at first because, Gran and Glenda were not little, they were big. So, when I inquired more, she'd said, "from time to time he asks for big helpers too!" And of course, I believed her, because which child would not.

I'm smiling again as these beautiful memories that are flooding my brain, memories I'd forgotten. I feel as though I've had amnesia for the past 4 years, and my memory is just returning. I wiggle my nose in affection towards Glenda as she lights my candle, then Grans. The lights go dim and the flicker of candles now light the church, a few coughs from the congregation to clear throats before Deck the Halls starts in a rapturous chorus from the choir in the eves. I grin and pull in a happy, ever so happy emotional breath, then belt out the words, 'like a good un.' As gran would say. I sing every carol, every word, and hum every single note.

My heart feels released, as I remember fond beautiful memories. I squeeze grans hand smiling at her, and her face says it all. I look at Glenda who winks and nearly makes me laugh, and in Church of all places. I hold it in though, then as calmly as I can I release it and nearly blow my candle out.

Gran smiles again, seeing how happy I am and mimes, "Your

back, Abbie." And I nod towards her, knowing that I am.

Chapter 3

The carol service has ended although I didn't want it to. It was everything I'd hoped it would be. Well apart from Edward not being here, but I know that can't be helped. We leave Church, making our way down towards the deli. I feel that I've finally taken that turn and that I'm on the right path, one, that I have chosen this time, not one, that some else has chosen for me. I'm not sure if it's because I've been to Church, maybe I wonder. But I don't mean that I've had an epiphany or been enlightened, or anything like that, it's just that I feel at peace for once and I'm thinking nice thoughts. Maybe I have subconsciously made my peace with God.

My thoughts are suddenly distracted by children running past skidding on the path in front. I laugh out-loud watching them teasing each other and throwing snowballs. My arm threads through Grans as the path between the Church and deli is a little slippery. "Happy Abigail?" she asks. I nod. As we continue walking, and It's the most beautiful night. The sky appears dark blue with stars twinkling bright. Snow flutters down, and as my gaze turns towards the deli noticing the fairy-lights flickering in the trees next to the garden, I almost have to pinch myself to ensure it real. It's like the opening scene from a Dickens film, with Christmas and joy written all over it.

"Williams done a fantastic job in the garden don't you think so Glenda?" I say, turning to look at her.

"He has that!" she answers proudly.

"He always does." Gran adds. "Now Abigail is Edward coming later?"

"Yes. He said he'd make the deli later; he's had to go to the hospital to sort something out. And I know he's very fond of hot mince pies and mulled wine." I reply with a smile. And as we enter through the gate onto the path, I instantly notice the grotto. I turn my eyes to grans as I want to ask, but I don't need to ask as she's read my thoughts. She nods in approval before disappearing through the door with Glenda, leaving me with memories of my childhood.

The main part of the grotto is painted in red, with two small window frames painted green that sit either side of the black door with the number 25 set in the middle. A candle flickers in each window making it look and over hangs the front part painted in white giving the illusion of snow. As I push the small door open it creaks as I bend my head to go inside. Grandads rocking chair sits proudly in the middle with sacks of present around it. My hand strokes the arm of the chair and it rocks with a squeak making me swallow holding back tears as I picture him sat there in his red Santa suit and white beard. I can almost hear him,

"Ho, ho, ho, Merry Christmas, Abbie."

My eyes close, "I miss you Grandad." I mime, wiping a lone tear from my cheek, before stroking the chair one more time as if I was touching his arm saying, goodbye, and as I leave to join the others, I wonder why some places bring back stronger memories than other that they seem to have a presence. Grans waiting just inside the door as I enter.

"I miss him too, Abbie, but he's never far away." She whispers hugging me.

"I know gran." I reply raising my eyes slightly and glancing around the room, changing the subject as I know we are both emotional. "The room looks beautiful."

"Yes." She gestures pointing around. "William has surpassed himself this year."

"He always does."

"Hey that's my line." She replies before we both laugh softly knowing that we're both doing the same thing without admitting it to each other.

We're both suddenly startled as a voice carries itself loudly across the room almost piercing my eardrums.

"Well - dear me. Abigail. I don't see you for ages, and then here you are again twice, in as so many weeks." My eyes roll as I want to laugh, although I can't fathom why, is it down to her surprise or shock of seeing me again. But she continues to speak with a hint of apprehension in her voice, before looking over my shoulder towards the doors. "Where's that good-looking Doctor of yours?" She asks with that girlish blush appearing on her cheeks.

"He's coming later." I answer trying not to laugh and I was just about to add something else when I stop as I've spotted Miss wiggly arse beamer walking towards us, but then I do manage a very quick but weak smile knowing she's given up her own time to raise money for the children and to ensure the villagers have a nice Christmas eve. She stops in front of us.

"Mrs Baxter, it's so nice to see you." She remarks smiling through a cheese wide grin, nodding her head mechanically towards me. I repeat the same gesture back, as Glenda disappears into the kitchens. She's scanning the room and I know exactly who she's really looking for. So, before she can ask, I answer for her.

"He's not here." And with great delight I apply the same cheesy grin back towards her. Gran looks at me, then at Mrs Bracewell, who's looking back at gran, because they don't know about the flirting she was doing with Edward on our last visit. And with my comment, she nods her head again, and trots of towards the kitchens, but this time not wiggling her arse as there's no one of any significance to see her. I smile internally noticing the Mistletoe over the door, and I can't help but wonder if she'd put it there just for chance. She really is I think an optimist, as I watch her disappear through the door, and back into the kitchen from where she came.

"So, gran where do you want me, behind the counter serving, or clearing the tables?" I ask, still smiling at my win with Miss Beamer.

"The counter I think dear." She replies still looking at me a little confused, then at the kitchen door, before turning her eyes back towards me, "Oh…and on the shelf under the till you'll find your hat, and scarf."

"My hat and scarf?" I reply quizzically.

A gold bell sits on the tip instead of the white pom-pom as it fell of some years earlier. Two bobbles fall from the hat. My memories are on flood alert as I know what I must do next. I part my hair and place it quickly into two pigtails then loosely plait it as Gran used to do for me when I was little, and then I remember

Edwards face while he stared at the photo of me with my hair in plaits. He did seem to like that photo, and said, 'he'd like to see me in pigtails now.' I blush wondering why? Then grin, because I know why, and that's why I blushed. The hat goes on, the scarf wrapped around, and I'm ready, dressed in festive attire stood behind the counter waiting to meet my customers. Before long I'm rushed of my feet. I've a little dish on the counter for the donation to the children's home as everything is free tonight, although I've had to set a plastic tub up as well, because people are being ever so generous with money, not just coins but notes.

I'm having such a wonderful time.

The doors fly open every now and again as children keep running outside to see if Father Christmas has arrived yet, but the breeze is welcomed as I'm quite warm. My cheeks are red and rosy. My jumper's far too warm for the deli and I'm wishing now I'd put a t-shirt on underneath, but Edward had insisted I got wrapped up so as not to get a chill, and I was already running late. So, I just pulled on the jumper as I'd no time to argue with him, although it wouldn't have done any good as he likes to get his own way, but he did justify it by saying, 'he's looking after me,' which I suppose I can cope with. So, dressed in my Aran cable thick wool jumper, black legging, thick socks and boots. I'm sort of melting and the scarf is adding to my glow and the hat is irritating me now making my head itch as I'm sweaty.

I've checked my phone several times in-between customers to see if he's texted or rang to say he's on his way. But he hasn't and I've not texted back or rang knowing he'd arrive when he can.

Suddenly shirks begin in a wave getting louder and louder, little bells start to jingle and a mass of shouting, giggling

and excitable children form a very wavy and wiggly line at the
door, because Gran has just announced Father Christmas has just
landed in his slay near to the Church and is making his way to the
grotto. My smile widens looking at their faces, their eyes almost
popping out of their heads, hearing shrieks of uncontrollable
excitement, them squirming trying to stay in line. This is what it's
about, the children it's delightful. Parents have now joined the
wiggly and not so orderly que near to the door that leads out to
the gardens. Gran nods at Glenda who in turn opens the door and
the children run quickly outside, as I slump into one of the chairs,
exhausted and hot taking a deep breath and wondering whether
the parents feel as excited or as happy as their children do. I know
I would feel so very excited if one of those children were mine. I
start to imagine holding their hand, giggling with them and
encouraging that magical feeling. I close my eyes almost seeing
myself in the line-up until a voice makes me open them. "Miss,
for you" I turn my attention to the voice, and I'm shocked as a
glass of mulled wine and a hot mince pie is placed in front of me,
by no less than Miss Beamer. I acknowledge the gesture with a
nod, before she walks off. I sip the wine and eat which I have to

say is delicious. My cheeks are still rosy and warm as I pull the hat of and loosen the scarf, my feet ache but my smile is still planted firmly across my face as I close my eyes entranced by Mr Bublé's dreamy voice serenading me in the background, but it doesn't last more than a nanosecond, before I jump as cold lips touch mine, then an equally smooth voice whispering into my ear,

"What are you doing to me with these pigtails, Baxter?" the voice murmurs, before a gentle tug of one. "you do know now what I'm going to have to do to you when I get you home." I grin with a tingle inside reaching my hand to his face that's almost touching mine. My eyes open to reveal a very seductive look in his eyes.

"Well Scott, you'll have to wait, because we've a lot of tiding up to do first before we can go home." He shakes his head holding out his hand to me. I shake my head back, his eyes raise, I squeal as he picks me up from my chair, then starts carrying me towards the door. "Edward put me down." Gran and Glenda are laughing as he plonks me on my feet then points upwards. I look up seeing the Mistletoe hanging over the door.

"It's the law, you have to kiss me."

"The law, really, I'd not realised Edward. I don't want to break the law." His head shakes as though to say, 'no you don't,' then Glenda shouts,

"Oh, Abbie, for God sake put him out of his misery and kiss him."

I turn laughing at them as their all stood watching, he nods in agreement. I reach up onto my tiptoes to kiss him on the lips, but he grabs me firm around the waist lifting me from the ground kissing me hard on the mouth and a little too long. I feel the blush deepen on my cheeks, as I'm aware that everyone is staring.

"Put me down, now."

"No. One more kiss then I will."

Which I must, because I know he'll not let me go until I do. So, I kiss him again to a roar of laughing and cheering from the room that has now started to get busy again, with parents and children. I hear children giggling and saying,

"Abbie, loves Edward." Their voices are mischievous but innocent, although I know it's true, that Abbie does love Edward even if he does embarrass her in front of everyone. He's smirking so much as I pull away.

"Love the pigtails babe," he teases running a finger down my cheek, "you're very flushed and warm." My eyes roll and I don't reply because his tone is over suggestive. So, he tugs again at the pigtail, "umm… and keep these in," he whispers making my blush deepen even more.

I nod not wanting to encourage him any further, especially in front of a packed room which of course he plays too. His tone returns to normal as his hand reaches out to Glenda who's just passed him a plate of warm mince pies and a mug of hot mulled wine.

"Thank you, Glenda." She simpers.

"Oh, if William was not here my lad, I'd cover you in lipstick under that Mistletoe." She remarks in a gruff voice. Edward laughs, as I nearly choke because William is here and making his way in through the door and over to us.

"So, my lad, you're the chap who is responsible for putting that perpetual smile back on our Abbie's face." He say's reaching out his hand. Edward places his plate and drink on the table before taking William's hand to shake.

"It's not hard, as I think you'll know making her smile.

And loving her, well that's easy." He says addressing everybody who's in ear shot.

I just stare rather taken aback by his remark. He really does say what he means. He turns and winks, before William replies.

"Good answer…. you'll do for me." And with that he walks past with Glenda in tow towards the kitchens, leaving me pleased, happy and totally gobsmacked once again. I can hear Glenda talking.

"I told you he was a nice boy and ever so good for her. She's not stopped smiling since she arrived at the Church."

"That's nice to hear she deserves a good un, especially after that rat. I'd love to see him Glen, God I'd make him pay for the things he's done to our, Abbie."

"I know William, but she's rid of him now."

"I she is that." Then silence as they enter the kitchen.

My eyes raise at Edward knowing he's just heard the same conversation as me. He winks again and puts his arm around me.

"What's left to do?"

"Just the clearing up and then home."

"I'll just finish my mince pie, and I'll give you a hand."

"Thank you. Did you get everything sorted at the hospital?"

He nods, but it's not his normal nod of his head, it's as though he doesn't want to talk about it or tell me what's happened. I don't think much about it wondering if he's finally winding down and switching off ready for the Christmas break. So, I don't ask any more questions.

"I'll just get a bag for the rubbish and start clearing up." He's staring at me fondly, "What?"

"Nothing, Abbie."

As I make my way around the room glancing back towards him, I've noticed he's just finished a call, but his eyes don't move from mine he's watching me, and I'm wondering if he's okay? something seems to be bothering him, but he doesn't want to tell me, or he doesn't want to tell me here. I smile back at him as I'm collecting the rubbish, but he nods raising his eyes slightly. I hope it's not his Grandad again, but surely, he would have told me that. I walk over speaking, "hey, what's the matter, is something bothering you Edward, you seem to be distracted."

"No, sweetheart I'm fine. I'm just tired that's all."

Although now I'm not convinced, I think something is bothering

him. I can tell, but what I don't know.

"Is your Grandad, okay?"

"Yes, he's fine. Stop worrying, Abbie. I'm okay?"

leave it, knowing if he wants to tell me he will, although

on the other hand it's probably work, maybe bad news from the

hospital private and confidential that he can't share. My eyes raise

internally knowing that I'm over analysing. So, I smile at him as

he comes to join me to finish tiding the room.

We're finished, the kitchens are returned to normal. All

the staff including Mrs Bracewell left earlier by taxi's provided

by Gran, leaving, Gran, Glenda, William and us alone. William

brings out the whiskey bottle and glasses, "I think a nip of

Whiskey before we leave?" He says gesturing for us all to sit

while he places the glasses and bottle on the table.

"Not for me thanks, William, I'm driving."

"I'll drive Edward if you want, I don't mind you have a

drink."

"No Abbie, I'd prefer to drive. The snows coming down and I'd not want us to get stuck in it. If you want a drink have one."

"No, I'm not fond of Whiskey."

"No, you've never liked the smell or taste of it have you." Gran adds. I just shake my head knowing what the smell reminds me of. So, on that note I ask Edward,

"Have we to make tracks then, if you think the snow is getting bad?"

"Do you mind?" I shake my head. Gran asks if we'd remembered the time for lunch tomorrow, as we put on our coats. We all hug each other, and Glenda ensures she sneaks a little kiss from Edward before we leave making us all raise are eyes, apart from Glenda that is who looks pleased as punch.

Chapter 4

We leave the warmth of the deli into the cold Christmas eve night. Snow covers the ground, and there's an icy nip in the air as the wind whips through the tree branches blowing large white snowflakes into the air before they land gracefully onto the path. It's pretty to watch but rather cold and I'm thankful as Edward places his warm hand in mine and starts guiding me at a steady pace towards the car commenting as he goes.

"Come on, let's get a move on or we could get stuck."

"It's not that bad just a dusting. I'm sure the Beast can handle it."

"Yes, it can, but the roads coming in were quite snowy, plus the road at home is a little deep in parts."

I look at him puzzled by what he's just said because they didn't seem that bad when we left.

"Oh, have you been home then before coming here tonight?"

"No, I came straight from the hospital."

I don't answer wondering why he's said he came straight from the hospital, when it's clear to me he's not. He's come from the house, or how would he know about the road being deep in parts with snow. I'm confused, but there again I don't want to push him into an answer or to ask why he's lying to me. So, I stare out of the window instead keeping my thoughts to myself.

The gates open on to the drive and we drive through up towards the house. There are lights flashing as we approach. I look at him and he seems tense, his window goes down, and I hear an alarm blasting as we approach closer, he pulls the Beast to a stop and the tyres screech before skidding in the snow. His seatbelt is whipped off quickly as he shouts.

"Stay in the car!"

"What. No, I'm coming with you."

"For once do as your bloody told and stay in the car!" He snaps again before jumping out and locking me in. I'm stunned, he's never raised his voice like that - well not at me. He looked scared as he spoke and I'm now worried as I see him disappear through the door leaving it open. The lights are still flashing, the alarm is still sounding, and my hands begin to tremble, because I don't know what's happening. God, anything could have happened. My mind whizzes with all the possible scenarios. What if someone is inside the house? What if they hurt him and I'm sat here doing nothing? I quickly pull the car door open and start running towards the entrance entering the hallway where I can hear him speaking, his voice is shaky. I run down the hall not thinking just wanting to get to him, calling his name. He stops abruptly as he hears my voice then sees me coming into the kitchen. He immediately stops talking, holding his phone to the side before shouting his words.

"I told you to stay in the car."

He looks panicked. I freeze seeing Shadow on the floor, he's not moving and blood covers the floor to the side of his head, a gust of wind hits me from the smashed window in the door and my hand flies to my mouth as I run towards the dog crushing glass beneath my feet before kneeling at his side, he whimper's. Edward's back on his phone almost shouting at the person on the other end,

"On my way now!" He ram's the phone back into his pocket before moving forward and picking Shadow up from the floor, he whimper's again. Blood is coming from his head and I notice Edwards hands and clothes are blood stained. He glares at me speaking firmly, "Get in the car, now!"

I move out of his way quickly and practically run down the hallway to make my way through the door waiting for Edward to catch up, slamming the it shut behind us. I continue running ahead to open the car door to the backseat where Edward gently lays him. It's serious. Shadow appears lifeless and I'm praying he doesn't die as I clamber into the back with him. He snaps,

"Get in the front and put your seat belt on."

I shout back I think out of pure fear, and I know Edward doesn't mean to snap because he's just as upset and scared as I am.

"No, I'm staying with him."

My door closes before he gets in the driver's seat moving quickly off, and the Beast skids in the snow. He doesn't speak and appears tense. So, I continue to stroke Shadow carefully talking softly to him.

"Come on, good boy, you keep your eyes open and look at me," his head moves slightly towards my voice, "Good boy. Edward, what on earth has happened?" He doesn't answer but concentrates on driving. We pass the town and enter up the main road towards the police station. He pulls the car to an abrupt halt just outside, removes his seatbelt, and everything seems to be in double time as he practically jumps from the car. I seem to be on auto pilot knowing what he wants me to do as I open the back door for him to take the dog. We start to run towards the entrance and in through the doors to the reception area where there's a man waiting.

"This way Ed." We follow him through the glass reception area then on through a door towards the back of the station. "He's on his way, I've called Mathew."

Edward doesn't reply. Another door is opened to a room which appears to look like a theatre room. It must be the vet's area for the police dogs. Edward places Shadow on the table before grabbing some gloves puts them on before parting the dog's fur to examine the wound. His eyes close briefly and I can tell he's holding back tears as he sees it for the first time, it looks deep and he's lost a lot of blood. Edward turns to look at me as I suck in my lips not wanting to appear shocked, because I know there is nothing I can do or say to make it better.

"Simon, please take Abbie, into the reception."

"I want to stay."

His head shakes and Simon guide's me out. I hear Edward talking to Shadow with a muffled broken voice that sounds full of tears. He's telling him to fight, and to be strong.

"What's happened Simon, who's done this?"

His expression is vague as though I should know who's done this and what has happened, but I don't, and he doesn't tell me.

"Please, Abbie, just sit there and wait for Edward, I'm sure he'll tell you." His voice is sincere, it reminds me of Edwards voice with the same tone, the same accent that's reassuring, but strangely his words are not making me feel reassured.

A door opens. Simon turns and starts speaking to the person entering.

"Mathew this way, please." I look towards Mathew he's carrying a black bag and I'm presuming Mathew, is the vet.

"Thank you for coming." He gestures with his hand holding another door open.

"It's fine Simon. I was on call anyway tonight being Christmas eve. Police dogs need vets as well as coppers needing doctors." He comments factually before disappearing through the door with Simon, leaving me sat on my own, not knowing what's happening, or who did this to Shadow, or if he's going to even live. I feel as though I've just switched the television on, and a film is on halfway through, and I don't know the plot or who the characters are. In fact, I feel pretty much lost and helpless to the situation.

Tears are in my eyes; my lip trembles and my hands won't stop shaking. I'm remembering Shadows eyes this evening on the stairs, they were alert and bright, but tonight they looked like coal, dark with no life in them. I pull in a sob, as my mobile starts to ring in my bag. I take it out, but my hands are still shaking as I answer sniffing and trying to stop my tears, but a snigger stops me almost immediately,

"I never hurt the fucking dog; he did that all by him-self trying to get to me through the window. But I'm glad it's hurt, because it bit my fucking ankle." I'm staring at the phone, dumb struck. Why, how, why Shadow? "And this is all your fault.

I've had a letter from the solicitors about the house, did you seriously not think I'd do something like this?"

I'm silent. I can't speak, it's as if I've something in my throat that's stopping my brain from answering. I'm confused as to how he knew where I was, and how he's got my number.

"You've got something of mine from the cellar and I want it back." I've no idea what he's talking about.

"What. How have you got this number and why have you done this?" That's all I can focus on saying.

"Because I can, and I'm very resourceful… you're still my wife, and you want a divorce!" He goes silent, then yells. "Never…I'll bury you first!" I drop the phone, glaring at it, as he screams at me from the floor. And despite his threats that are catapulting around my head, my thoughts are with Edward and Shadow. Not him or his fowl nasty words. My eyes close, trying to block him out, because I'm desperate for Edward to come through that door. I want him to walk in with Shadow. I want to see his tail wagging. I want to see his eyes bright. I want Adam to disappear from the face of the earth, but as I try my best to imagine this but all I can hear is him still screaming, demanding and threatening. I pull in a deep breath and practically snatch my phone from the floor.

"Adam." I screech, my face almost twisted with repulsion towards him.

"Oh, I've got your attention now, have I." He responds calmly but still with an air of aggression.

"No." I snap bluntly. I feel a gush of anger and almost spit my next words back at him. "But I will tell you this. Don't ring me, don't speak to me, and never, ever, come to Edwards house again, because if you do, I'll kill you, as God is my witness I'll do it, and if you kill me first then at least I'll die knowing I tried to rid the world of you!"

He laughs like the callous bastard he is, but I don't care and if he thinks I'm bluffing... I'm not. This is how he makes me feel. Nothing. I feel absolutely nothing for him, in fact he's already dead to me. I end the call, and then surprisingly place my phone back into my bag and sit astounded at myself for doing what I've just done, but then I remember what he said. 'Shadow bit him', it's been snowing, his blood will be kept fresh in the snow. I'm nodding my head, yes, we can prove he's been at the house, that it was him. I'm getting a little excited by the fact that I'm finally going to be able to pin something on him. I need to let Simon know. I need to tell him what Adam has just said to me, while the blood is still fresh.

The door opens and Edward walks out, our eyes meet but his look red and sad. I almost jump to my feet walking quickly towards him, his arms go around me tightly,

"I'm sorry sweetheart for shouting at you." I shake my head knowing I'd forgot about it already.

"How's Shadow?"

"Mathews operating on him now, he's lost a lot of blood and the wounds deep, but it's not pierced anything, so I suppose that's at least one good thing." I nod, not knowing quite what to say. "Listen Abbie, I want you to ring your Gran and tell her I'm going to drop you of there tonight." I shake my head, "No. I'm not going I'm staying with you." His eyes close, and I'm not sure what he's thinking. "Listen, please Edward. I want to stay with you and Shadow, and…" I pause looking at him as his eyes reopen, I continue apprehensively not at all sure how he's going to react, or if I should really be telling him this right now.

"I know who's done this."

His expression suddenly changes, one eyebrow arches as the other falls, his eyes have narrowed, his appearance and body language are inquisitive as to how I know this information, it's as if he himself knows, but I'm not meant too.

"And how do you know this?" he finally says slowly. I just stare, wondering whether to tell him or not, I'm unable to read him as I normally can. His expression remains static and his tone was flat.

"Adam."

"And how do you know it was Adam?" I'm now wondering if he already knew it was Adam, because he seems to be to calm at asking me that questions.

"I just do!" His eyes raise this time and I know he's not going to let it drop until I've told him how I knew it was him. "He rang my phone a few minutes ago and told me it was him who'd tried to break into the house. He said that I'd got something of his from the cellar, but I've not, and I've no idea what he was talking about."

"When did he ring you?"

"Like I said a few minutes ago."

"Can I have your phone." He asks holding out his hand.

I reach into my bag, removing it and handing it to him, but for some strange reason I don't ask why, I just give it to him, and he places it into his pocket.

"How has he got your number?" I shrug. "Who have you given your number to?" My eyes raise, does he think I've given him the number. He notices, and I think he knows what I'm thinking. "Well?"

"My gran, Alison." His eyes raise making me stop. "Don't be daft, Alison would never give him my number, and certainly if he approached her, she'd tell me." His eyes close briefly in admission to my answer, however this makes me cross that he'd think my friend would do that. "The Doctors, the deli, the bank, Oh…and of course…You!" His expression says what he's thinking, which I can read, it's saying, don't be ridiculous even thinking it was me. Which of course I don't think for one minute, but he's got to understand that what he's saying, or implying is also ridiculous.

"Edward. Did you know it was Adam?" He doesn't

answer. I'm staring at him as things seem to be slotting into place, as if I'm doing a jigsaw puzzle in my head. "Was it him in the garden tonight, the footprints. Was it him before?" My head is starting to spin as the pieces are slotting into place. I'm remembering all the weird stuff that at the time didn't mean very much to me, but now they do, and I need answers which I think Edwards got. "You've not been at the hospital, have you?" he breathes in. "Did he follow Ted, is that how he knew where I was. Is that how he's got my number. Is that why you've been acting the way you have? Because you've known all along it was him... stalking me!"

His eyes close briefly because he knows I've worked it out and he's going to have to tell me. He breathes in again but this time deeply and points back towards the chairs gesturing with his hand for me to sit. We both sit, and he starts to tell me what's been happening, about his suspicions. I'm shocked when he tells me that he found a pen drive on the floor in the cellar. I frown then remember him bending down and putting something into his pocket in the cellar, but I also remember him telling me that it was the car keys he'd dropped, and I thought nothing of it at the time. I rub my face with my hands.

"I'm sorry I never told you. I didn't want to freak you out until I was certain, does that make much sense?"

I'm not sure if I feel cross at him for not telling me.

"What have you done with the pen drive?"

"Simon has got it."

"And what's on it?" He shrugs. I'm a little put out, because I feel now that he's treating me like a child. "I'll ask again. What is on it." He's silent. "Tell me, it must be something important if he wants it back so desperately." He looks towards the floor still not speaking. "I thought you wanted no secrets Edward, or does that only apply to me?"

"It wasn't nice stuff, Abbie. I was trying to protect you."

"From what?"

"Him. He's one sick fucking bastard."

"What do you mean?"

"I don't want to tell you; I think you've been through enough."

I close my eyes getting frustrated, because I need to know. I think I've a right, but deep down I understand what he's done by not telling me, although, he's going to tell me, because I must know.

"That is for me to decide don't you think." He's silent as if he's struggling to come to terms with telling me.

"Okay, but you're not going to like it. On the drive were films of woman being abused and hurt.".

"So, he was watching them?" he shakes his head and the look in his eyes tells me and confirms what he knows. "You mean it was him taking part." He nods,

"It sounded like him, but we couldn't see his face, only the woman's face." I put my hand up,

"Stop, I don't wish to know, you're right. He's sick. And Simon can he do anything with the pen drive." He shakes his head again in defeat.

"We can't prove any off it. You were right Abbie, he's clever and covered all his tracks, and the club we presume could be absolutely any basement." I shrug my shoulder, thinking, basement, pen drives, sex clubs, hitting, torturing woman for pleasure. I stand and he takes my hand standing with me and I just stare at his face feeling ashamed, disgusted, and utterly,

utterly, naive although that's probably not the right word to describe how blind, stupid and totally gullible I've been. I never knew any of this, what he was doing. What he was doing to woman, but it explains his behaviour towards me. And the things he'd done, making me cry while he…. I stop myself, because I don't need to think those thoughts anymore. I stare at his eyes and there sincere. So, I nod, as he gently smiles and he knows I'm not mad with him and that I know why he didn't tell me, because he wanted to protect me. Edward and Adam are poles apart. And I'm certainly not allowing Adam to chip away at me ever again.

"I know why you did it Edward and that we can't prove any off the other stuff, but I think we can prove that it was him tonight who tried to break into your house."

"How?"

"The phone call." He nods continuing to listen. "He told me that Shadow had bitten his ankle." His eyes raise, and I know he's thinking the same thing as me.

"You're thinking blood Abbie, in the snow?" I nod, he smiles. "Umm… we might be on to something there."

"Will we need to go to the house to get D…" I stop

talking as the door opens and we both turn our heads towards Mathew as he walks through. His face looks pale. We both stare at him waiting anxiously for news.

"He's going to make it, but he needs to stay in at least overnight. The bleedings stopped, and I've put up fluid. I suppose you want to see him." We both nod and follow Mathew back through the door to Shadow.

Chapter 5

Shadows eyes are closed as he lays curled up on a soft cushion with a blanket placed over him. His head has a dressing on which is tied with a bandage. A drip is attached to his front paw, he looks comfortable and more settled then he did only a few hours ago. Edward walks slowly over, then kneels at his side, stroking him gently across his back, whispering,

"Well done, boy." His head moves slowly towards his voice. It's moving to watch the bond between them, and for the first time in hours, Edward smiles, and that smile makes things better. I'm holding my hand to my chest thanking God, he's alright, then Mathew for saving him. Edward returns to his feet and thanks him with a handshake.

"Let him rest now, come back in the morning." Mathew says before releasing Edwards hand. He nods and takes hold of my hand before leading me out through the door and back into the reception.

"Just sit a minute please, there's something I need to do before we leave."

I've been sat for a short time and not really thinking about anything as my mind seems to be blank. Edward walks through the door talking with Simon.

"Thanks Simon. I don't think he would have made it if you had not let us bring him here tonight."

"Hey, he used to be one of ours, and a good police dog at that before his accident." He answers patting Edward on the shoulder. "Are you still going to Mum and Dads on Boxing day?"

I stare at Edward waiting for him to reply, because I'd not thought of that, or thought about going to my grans tomorrow as things may have changed now. Edward looks at me then back towards Simon.

"We'll speak, I'm sure we can sort something out."

"Please don't make any decisions on what you think I might want to do, honestly what-ever you decide to do, it's fine with me."

"But your Grans tomorrow?"

"It's fine, I can sort that. You just do what you think's best."

He squeezes my hand and I immediately see his expression change as a light relief reflects in his eyes.

"I'll sort something out about Boxing Day and then I'll ring Mum, tomorrow."

Simon just nods. It's obvious they know each other well, but of course they're brothers after all. I look at Simon, then back towards Edward. They're very much alike and I'm struggling to see the differences between them. They could be twins, although I think Simon is older. He looks older in his early thirties. His suit is immaculately fitted over his tall strong physique. He's a little shorter than Edward but only fractionally. He's clean shaven with that same sharp jaw line and chin. His hair is cut shorter and his eyes are dark blue. He's extremely handsome.

"Okay, no problems." His tone and manner are confident, exactly the same as Edwards it makes everyone sit up and listen. He reaches out with his hand to me and I notice his wedding ring as I take it to shake.

"It was nice to meet you Abbie, at last. I just wish it was under better circumstances." He smiles softly, and as I stare at his smile, I suddenly realise what's different about them. Their smile.

When Edward smiles at me it makes me feel safe. It

makes me feel loved and makes me feel as if I'm the only person in the world that matters to him. And of course, it makes me blush. Plus, from what I've seen it makes everybody blush who encounters it. Men as well as woman. People take notice of his face. Woman blush letting him know what they're thinking, what they'd like him to do to them. Men want to be him. He's charismatic, alluring, confident, well-structured in his position, and at the forefront of his game.

I stare at him now wondering what he's doing with me. Why me? When he could have absolutely any woman he desired. But he wants me. Me with my messed-up life and all my problems. He made that perfectly clear to me the day I went home with him from the hospital. Saying,

'He'd never felt so scared, or alone when I'd collapsed, that he knew he loved me from the first time he saw me. I was like a drug that he couldn't get enough of.' He made me laugh. But he was serious and continued, 'He was a one-woman man now that he'd found me, and that '**yes**' he did mate for life. I raised my eyes, remembering that day so well. The day he brought me home and what I thought about the swans when he told me that they mated for life, and I remember thinking: 'Did he mean the swans or him?'

He said it again, confidently,

'Yes, Abbie, like the swans …forever, together.'

And I do sometimes wonder if he can read my thoughts. He's not only beautiful on the outside but internally as well. I need to pinch myself daily to remind me that I've found my soul mate, my Swan.

Simons talking to Edward, but I wasn't listening to what they were saying. I was thinking about Edward and how blessed I feel to have the love of this extraordinary man.

"See you later Edward. Bye, Abbie."

"Oh, yes. Bye, Simon." I add a little faintly feeling a bit rude that I was not paying attention to their conversation. He nods back towards us both as Edward takes my hand and leads us both through the door and towards the car.

"Are you okay?"

"God, yes…Sorry, are you?"

"I am." I know now what belongs to him is his. He's so protective and will protect what is his no matter what.

I wonder if that is how he sees me. That I belong to him, but if he does, I'm not at all bothered, because I like belonging to him. In fact, I want to belong to him.

We enter the house and start making our way to the kitchen as I know there's a lot of cleaning up to do. The door flies open to the laundry and a man comes out. I'm startled not knowing who it is. He's standing there in a pair of blue checked pyjama bottoms, and what looks like army boots with the laces not fastened. He's tall and slender with an athletic build. He's wearing a long-sleeved blue t-shirt pushed up at the arms. He's the appearance of a soldier standing there, his hair is cut into an orderly crew cut. But again, he also looks like he's just got out of bed. He swings the hammer in his hand as I stare at him,

"Edward, the doors secure." He says, almost churning out the words like a military command. My eyes turn abruptly to Edwards. He's shaking his head at me.

"Abbie, this is Jimmy." His eyes return to Jimmy. "Cheers mate, but It could have waited until the morning."

"It's fine Edward, it's better to have this door secure." He confirms this with a firm nod of his head.

I glance towards the door which has now got a wooden board over it instead of the pane. The glass on the floor has been cleared up, and apart from the wood on the door you might not ever guess what has happened in here tonight. Jimmy turns back towards me.

"Sorry, did I scare you? You must be Abbie, pleased to meet you. I'm Jimmy, as Edward said." I lift my eyes, a little taken aback. Never in a million years would I have guessed this was Jimmy, the gardener, with talented nimble fingers. Hell, I nearly saluted him when he spoke, and his age, I was expecting someone a lot older, but he looks like he's in his early thirties give or take a few years.

"Hi, Jimmy." I manage eventually, before staring back at Edward. Then I remember my manners. "It's nice to meet you too and thank you for clearing everything up." I gesture with my hand around the room. "Its very kind of you…."

My sentence has been cut short by the distraction of my phone ringing in Edwards pocket. He removes it looking at the screen then starts walking out from the kitchen and down the hallway. I glare at Jimmy as Edward answers then bellows.

"You, fucking! ring her again, and God, help you… I'll find you and break every bone in your body."

He's gone quiet, as the caller must be saying something back. I walk further out into the hall, his back is to me and every muscle seems tense, I know who the caller is. There is only Adam who could make Edward respond like this.

"I bet you do, you're a sick bastard, but I'm telling you this just once. If you ever go near her, speak to her, or even breathe on her. I'll know. And that pen drive you're so desperate to get back I'll plaster it all over social media. So, I suggest you fuck off, and crawl back into that hole where you belong."

He presses end and rams the phone into his pocket out of temper. He turns seeing me standing there in total shock.

"You can have your phone back, when I get you a new sim." I nod. "You can take mine if you like for now." He hands me his phone. "I'm sorry you heard that." But honestly, I'm struggling for something to say in response, because I think I'm a little worried that he meant it.

"God, this is such a mess Edward, and I'm so sorry he did that to Shadow. This is my fault I should never have antagonised him."

His eyes fly to mine; he looks cross at me for saying what I've just said.

"No, Abbie, he should take heed now, because he should have never done those things to you. And he certainly shouldn't antagonise me."

I put my hand on his arm.

"Look, I love you, but I don't want you tangled up with him because of me."

"We're not going to waste any more time or breath over him. I'm taking control now, so, if you hear from him, or he rings you, you tell me. Promise me." I nod. "Good girl. Come on, I think we need to let Jimmy get off home. And then bed."

As were walking back into the kitchen, I glance at his face, knowing everything he does is for me, and for my benefit to take care of me. He's so protective, but that's how it should be. I don't feel scared anymore of Adam, or frightened, because I know he'll not do anything now. Especially after what Edward just said to him, and there's one thing I do know about Adam, and that is, he's a bully. I bet not many people have stood up to him in the past, he's probably got everything his own way. Well, we're on to him, and one step ahead, and he knows it. So, I think he'll back off. He doesn't know Edward, but I think he's starting too, because even if you can't see his face on the pen drive, he'll not want to take that chance.

We're both stood at the door seeing Jimmy out. He holds out his hand for me to shake with a little sympathetic smile. I think he still feels guilty for scaring me. "Night Abbie, and sorry again for making you jump."

"It's fine don't worry about it." Then there's a long pause from them both. I feel as if I'm not wanted now, that they want to say something without me hearing, so, I take my cue to leave making an excuse up that it chilly. "I'll leave you if you don't mind? It's a little chilly stood here at the door." Jimmy smiles, as Edward nods, but I think they know it was a fib. I make my way down the hall back towards the kitchen, but as I'm entering, I hear Edward.

"I'll see you out Jimmy." They both seem to walk out through the door onto the steps probably so that I'm out of ear shot, this confirms to me that they did want to speak alone.

I can't make out what Edward says, although Jimmy's reply is loud enough.

"Do you want me to sort the fucker out, Ed?"

There quiet again. then I hear Edward,

"Night Jimmy." The door closes then locks; his footsteps get louder before entering the kitchen. He smiles, I discreetly raise my eyes, wondering if Jimmy is really the Gardner. Or, Edwards personal hit man?

"We could have asked him to stay, Edward." I comment passing him a drink and pretending I'd not heard any of the conversation. He shakes his head. "But it's Christmas eve, he's on his own."

"That's how he likes it."

"What, being on his own?"

"Yes, he's a bit of a loner."

"Oh," I reply, because I get the impression that Edward doesn't want to say any more than that, and really, it's not the time or place to pursue it.

"Come on, I think bed is in order."

"Yes."

We take our drinks to bed and we're sat up against the headboard still talking.

"Abbie, how do you think Adam, got your number?" I shrug

"I've no idea, honestly, but he did say, 'he was resourceful.' what-ever that meant."

"He did, did he?" I nod to confirm, but he's silent which always makes me wonder what he's thinking. He's that look again on his face as if he's working something out, but to be frank I don't ask, because Adam has my number, but Edward has my phone and the sim is being changed so, that's the end of that. But the one thing that is nagging me is the pen drive. I want to ask Edward what he's seen on it, yet again I don't, because... do I really want to know. I'd love to see if I could make out his face and identify him, but I don't want to see him doing the things he's doing. I sigh quite loudly.

"Are you alright?"

"Yeah, it's just the pen drive that's nagging me. I'd love to prove it was him, but I don't want to watch it? Does that make sense."

"Yes, of course it does. I know what you mean." I roll my eyes a little at the situation, because surprisingly I do feel okay. I'm not shocked which at first, I thought I would be, but I've realised, nothing or everything Adam does, or doesn't do, doesn't shock or surprise me anymore. I've done a little research on Narcissistic behaviour as Mrs Bradshaw had suggested, and he fits the bill to a T. It's not me who's crazy, it's not me who has the flaws, he distorted my reality. Brutalised, abused and tried to destroy my life to ensure that other people saw him as flawless. I know now for the past four years I've been looking at my life and the world through broken glass with no clear picture, and that's what he wanted, but my glass has now been replace and I see clearly. I see my life. And the world without Adam. Edward pats my knee bring me out of my thoughts.

"Are you sure you're okay?"

"Yes, sorry, my heads swimming now."

"Of course, it is, it's a big thing for you to decide. Don't make a decision now, think about it, what you want to do, and I'll support you either way." Edward is my clear glass, he's very logical and I wish I could be like that, although I do think I'm getting there.

"Was it horrible."

"Well, it wasn't nice, and not something I'm into… I don't mind a bit of kink" I raise my eyes. "but not hard-core stuff like that." I'm quiet and wonder what he meant by 'hard core stuff.' I suppose I am naïve. "He didn't do that…" My look stops him in his tracks. "Sorry I shouldn't have asked that." He replies quickly, and I know he was thinking out loud. It shows on his face that he's regretting mentioning it in the first place.

"Let's change the subject, please." I ask not wanting to remember anything Adam did. I'm trying to erase that from my memory… "Oh, I don't know, maybe I should just watch the bloody thing, get it over with, then I may not dwell on it." He shrugs, as I stare, but now he looks worried.

"The thing is Abbie…you know I'd not watched the pen drive when I spanked you, that it was later. Simon had seen it and asked me to watch it with him to see if I recognised him."

"Edward, I know I'd worked that out. I know you're not like him."

"I'm nothing like him." His remark is very defensive.

"I know, so don't beat you're self-up over it. You're poles apart, and you did it as you said, not to hurt me, but to give me pleasure. I freaked, yes at the time, but we spoke, ironed it out, and the pleasure you give me, is through love, and that's different." He rubs his hands over his face as though it's a relief. "Let's not talk about that again." he nods. "And I did say that we'd talk first, which we have, and that I was not all together against the idea." He nods in agreement remembering my words.

I snuggle down at his side. His arm comes around my waist, a kiss to my forehead, my eyes close, and surprisingly I fall asleep wrapped safely in his arms.

Chapter 6

It's Christmas day morning and I'm woken by Edwards voice as he speaks on his phone, his back is to me as he looks out of the French doors that lead out onto the balcony overlooking the ocean. He's only wearing his pyjama bottoms. I breathe in discreetly enjoying and admiring his manly physique, his strong broad back, powerful, muscular arms. A grin emerges across my face as I gape at his very perk bottom, and, yes, I feel blessed as I yawn and sit up in bed, almost drooling. A little shocked as for once I have a night dress on which living with Edward is a novelty and to be honest a rarity. He turns to face me, nods, acknowledging me with a smile, then thanks the person he's speaking to and hangs up.

I'm sleepy this morning although I have slept relatively well considering what has happened over the past twenty-four hours? I'm getting better at taking advice and help. Edward strides towards me, and I'm thinking *'our first Christmas together.'*

He grins, making me grin, and for some reason

I know it's good news. He looks as though a lead weight has been lifted from his shoulders.

"Shadow's coming home today. He's awake, ate breakfast and doing well by all accounts." This news brings a huge smile.

"I'm so pleased, what time can we pick him up?"

"About twelvish? I'm right in thinking were not at your grans until two." His voice has a bounce in it, and I feel he's back to his normal self. And I feel the same.

"Yes, Two o clock."

"Coffee, Edward?" I ask stretching out my arms and moving the duvet. He shakes his head with a gleam in his eye. My eyes raise, because I know what that gleam means, although I can't resist teasing him. "No. You don't want coffee?" I remark with a little shake of my head as though I'm shocked. "Orange juice then?" His head slowly moves from side to side replying silently, but seductively, 'no' then swiftly his pyjama bottoms are removed with ease and it's plain and simple to see exactly what he wants. "Oh, I see what you want." I remark with a hint of seduction.

He stares and doesn't speak making my pulse race especially with the hot look he's now giving me. He starts crawling up the bed on his hands and knees towards me. My heart nearly leaps from my chest, and it takes all my willpower not to squeal as I tingle all over in anticipation at what he's going to do.

I pant heavily as he grabs my ankles firmly, before pulling them towards him to ensure I'm flat on the bed. His hand darts up the inside of my thigh lifting my night dress at the same time and forcing my legs apart. He breathes huskily and I break out in goosebumps.

"You know what I want."

My head automatically nods. His mouth goes to my breast kissing and suckling through the silk. One hand grabs the material that's up around my hips as he tugs hard pulling it from my body. He's hungry to have me, and that stare as he   scans my naked body is so arousing, while his hands move quickly back to the inside of my thighs forcing them down onto the bed splaying them wide. His voice is husky,

"I want to taste you."

I nod with no words. His head lowers between my legs and my back arches from the bed as a moan of appreciation leaves my lips, and I know this is what I need.

"Keep still, while I take you with my tongue."

An inaudible noise leaves my lips that erupts screaming into my head and I know what my need is. I know I must do as I'm told and let him dominate me, because this way my reward will be far greater. My eyes roll as he starts the desirable assault, hungry and greedy taking me once more into a frenzy of goosebumps and tingles. My body is his. My desires are his. My need and my greed are his, and all at his command for his taking.

"Come for me, Abbie!" I obey feeling the burn through every nerve and blood vessel that almost makes me shake uncontrollably, and his remark is simple and confident, "Good girl," which leaves me gasping for breath as I climax while he continues moving his lips up my body before kneeling in front of me and wrapping my trembling legs around his waist. "Now, I'm going to fuck you."

I nod, knowing that he's my addiction. He's the drug that I can't get enough of. He sinks deep into me, taking me into our world, that world, once again of sublime pleasure.

I'm left breathless once again, a quivering wreck of emotion and sensation that floods my entire body and mind, he lifts himself on to his elbows his face almost touching mine, and whispers,

"Merry Christmas, beautiful."

"Merry Christmas, Edward." I beam, before he leaves the bed making his way to the ensuite as I curl up under the duvet, exhausted and feeling as if I'm going to float away on a cloud of pure white happiness. That's how Edward makes me feel. I stretch out my arms, knowing I need to get up before I fall asleep, but instead I yawn, then think, *five more minutes*. My smile widens as I hear Edward singing in the shower, he sounds so happy and at last chilled. I feel happy too, and I know I've come on leaps and bounds. And that's a very good feeling, because I know I've mended that part of my life. Although I do have to admit, Edward is a very good distraction, especially in the bedroom. He's so attentive to my needs. I giggle again like a daft schoolgirl, but it's a good giggle, and I'm becoming more acquainted with laughter and giggling by the day.

I suddenly scream as the duvet is ripped from me. His voice is stern, as I stare at his beautiful, gleaming, wet naked body. He smirks, rubbing his wet hair with a towel.

"God, woman are you going to lay-about in bed all day?" I throw the pillow but he's quick and dodges out of the way. "You need to be faster than that." He chuckles picking it up and throwing it back onto the bed. His voice was firm and he's certainly back to his normal, bossy, Neanderthal self, which I love so much. "Shower. Coffee. Breakfast. Presents" he churns out like a military command just like Jimmy did last night… a pause, a smirk, before he continues, "then we can pick up Shadow." I shake my head with a giggle, at this bossy Adonis. He pretends to be shocked. "No, really! Your saying no… to me?" I nod slowly. "Oh… I see Abbie, you want to do it again?" his head is cocked to one side with a huge grin planted across his face. I shake my head letting out a sigh, as though

I can't believe what he's just said.

"Do you not think about anything else?"

He doesn't reply but has a glint in his eye that confirms that he doesn't. He's blatantly staring at my naked body as I'm getting out of bed making my way past him, he makes a grab for my arm, but misses, I smirk.

"Ah, ah, ah I don't think so dear, you said shower."

I wiggle my finger in front of his face. His eyes widen and he's trying not to laugh. He grabs for my arm again catching it this time. I squeal as he nearly spins me pulling me into his chest. I place my hand on his wet skin.

"Edward, I'm going for a shower, you can make the coffee." His eyes are wide as though he can't believe what I'm saying. "Then you can make my breakfast, pick up shadow, before we do the presents."

I'm trying so much not to laugh, but of course he's nearly busted me, because a noise leaves my throat at the expression on his face. He taps my bum and the noise turns into a silly laugh. His eyes raise again, as he releases me from his hold.

"Bossy little bugger aren't you, all-of-a-sudden." I nod. "Okay." he adds pushing me towards the dressing room. "Go and get your shower." Then he slaps my bottom a little harder. I turn and glare with a raised eye. "What." He says all innocent. I huff, before turning with a smile and start walking towards the door with a very seductive wiggle. "I know what you're doing, Abbie" he mutters.

I turn back looking all innocent, "What?" I answer slowly using his words back at him. His voice is gruff as I know which buttons to press, so I continue with my wiggle to the door, my head I move slightly looking towards him before entering, then slowly blow him a kiss before shouting,

"If you can catch me, then you can have me."

He makes me jump and I scream as he practically runs towards me. My heart is now racing with excitement. My scream has turned into laughter as I'm running through the dressing room towards the bathroom. My hearts pounding so fast that I feel dizzy as he continues chasing me through the door. But I also feel just like your meant to feel when you're in love, and in love on the most magical day of the year. Christmas day!

Chapter 7

We enter back through the door with Shadow, and I must say he looks surprisingly well considering what's happened. I nod internally thinking, how resilient animals are compared to us humans. Granted he's not as bouncy as he normally is but his tail wags never-the-less when he sees his bed in front of the fire in the lounge. I wiggle my nose at Edward as he gets in his basket curling around making himself comfy.

"I'll make us coffee…then presents?"

"Yep, that sounds like a plan." He answers.

"What time's Jimmy coming?" I ask walking towards the door.

"About one-ish, is that okay?"

"Yep, that sounds like a plan to me!" I answer with a grin walking towards the kitchen.

As I return with coffees, Edward is just finishing laying all my presents on the sofa, his grin is wide as I pass him his drink.

"Heck… have you bought more?"

"Sit, Abbie and open them."

And I do with a smile, knowing he's bossy, but spoils me far too much. He hands me a large, slim, oblong box, tied with a ribbon.

"You're very nimbled fingered Edward, have you been taking lessons from Jimmy?"

I giggle at my own joke, but he just stares at my sarcasm as I remove the ribbon then the lid. Inside is cream tissue paper which I remove carefully to reveal a beautiful lace basque. My eyes raise as he grins, then winks.

"Thank you, it's beautiful."

"You're welcome… Abbie." He says slowly.

Present after present I've opened. Perfume, handmade chocolates, clothes, a very expensive wool black coat with the softest fur trim I've ever felt. A stunning bracelet in white gold with encrusted diamonds and earrings to match. A pair of designer leather boots in black with fantastic treads, they have the same fur trim as the coat. I realise there the same designer, Prada. I smile remembering the Drake, he nods, in agreement. "Edward it's too much." He shrugs,

"Well, why not, Abbie, they thought your jeans were Prada. Remember?"

"Yes, I do, remember."

"And the boots will stop you slipping on your arse."

I can't retort, not this time at his comment, because I'm too overwhelmed at the thoughtfulness of the gifts.

"Edward, you still shouldn't have, it's far too much."

He hands me the last present with a smirk. I open the carefully wrapped present to reveal yet another beautiful delicate lace basque which I take gently from the box as the lace work is exquisite.

"From Paris" he confirms with a sharp nod of his head.

"Wow, it's stunning…." I say feeling the soft lace between my fingertips. "I'd be too scared to wear it."

His eyes raise, and I know that it wasn't bought to look at in the box or in my hands, it was bought to be worn and admired. I get a little rush of tingles up my spine, and now I can't resist teasing him.

"Edward, are all, or most of my presents… I mean… do they have a dual purpose?" He winks, and his grin is wicked revealing the true nature of some of the presents.

"Umm…that has."

His eyes close as though he's imagining it and I feel a little creep of warmth flow over my cheeks. His eyes open and he sees.

"Blushing, stop it." A low growl leaves his throat, which makes me tingle again. "That white basque against your soft white skin."

I grin, shaking my head, knowing that my presents did have a dual purpose but to be quite-frank, I don't mind in the slightest.

"You can wear that tonight if you wish, or what about now. Try it on for size just to make sure it fits."

I laugh this time at his persistence but remain firm with my answer as I walk past and pat his arm just to let him know I've registered the thought, before kneeling and reaching under the tree to get his present and card.

"Then wait I shall." He replies slowly with a gleam in his eye. I nod passing him the card.

"Yes, Edward," I suddenly remember one line he used on me. "All good things come to those who wait." I bat back. He bows his head in acceptance and it's obvious that he recalls the line too. I stand and pass him the card to open first.

"Now please, your turn to open your present."

"I've got all the presents I ever want right here in front of me."

I nearly melt as he meant that. Then Shadow makes a noise which makes us both laugh as it sounds like, For goodness sake.

"Open the card first." I ask nervously. He opens it and sees the picture on the front of the Robin sat on the snowy white tree.

"You've already got me a card."

"Yes, but this is special, please open it and read the words." His eyes widen in curiosity. My heart is now jumping in my chest, because I'm hoping he likes what I've wrote, and as he begins, I silently read the words with him.

To my Edward,

Whenever I'm lonely, or feeling sad, or memories float over me that are bad. I close my eyes and picture your face, knowing my heart has reserved a place. A place for you that's made it whole.

You came like a thief into my life, and not only my broken heart you stole, but my lost and lonely soul. You're my friend, my love, my life, my dreams, Edward you're my everything. So, what I'm really trying to say, is I love you more with every day.

All my love, Abigail xxx

He's finished reading, and his eyes lift towards mine as I hand him the present.

"Please, open your present."

He starts to unwrap it to reveal the lush purple box with gold lettering reading, Rolex. He smiles as he opens the lid and removes the watch.

"Beautiful, Abbie," he says removing his own watch and going to put it on. I shake my head and he look's puzzled.

"Please, turn it over." My voice is shaky, and he knows. I've tears in my eyes from emotion. "Please." He nods, turning it over slowly to reveal the inscription, as I close my eyes and read once again with him,

Thank you for mending me! Abbie x

I open my eyes as his move to mine, they close slightly. I swallow down, as he walks over putting the watch onto his wrist grabbing me firmly and pulling me into his arms. He doesn't speak but cups my face gently with his hands staring right into my soul, and I feel his stare, it almost stops my heart from beating, and he doesn't need to tell me that he likes it, or that he likes my words, his eyes are telling me. He pulls in a deep breath,

"I'm speechless, Abbie."

"You are!"

"You have just blown me out of the water. My heart was actually racing as I read your word then the inscription...I've done that for you!"

I nod with a smile, knowing he has no idea at all what he's been doing for me.

"How. How have I done those things?" I smile, at his confused, but happy, face,

"By loving me the way you do. The little things, the big things, taking care of me, but mostly...for just being you!"

He still doesn't answer but keeps staring into my eyes. He breathes in.

"Thank you, Abbie, it's beautiful. I've never had words spoken or written for me like that. I'll treasure them both, far as long as I live, and most of all I'll treasure you!"

Oh God, I think I'm going to cry, because I've never had words like that spoken to me either.

"You're welcome Edward, and I mean every single word."

He takes my mouth so gently and meaningful, that I feel love radiating from him. We kiss and hug until Shadow barks, as Jimmy walks into the lounge. I move quickly away and stand at Edwards side. He places his arm around my shoulder. Shadows tail wags at seeing Jimmy and he smirks at us both,

"Sorry, should I have coughed before entering." He remarks with a laugh. "Hello boy." He says to Shadow walking over to him. "You look a lot better." Both Edward and I just stare at him. He grins again. "I thought I'd take Shadow to mine Edward, he's not right yet or he would have greeted me at the door as normal. If that's okay? and it would be easier for you both tomorrow." Edward nods back in agreement.

"Yes, take him to yours, cheers. Oh yes, and you should have coughed or knocked first."

"Sorry mate. I'm not used to you having female company around."

Edwards eyes raise with a grin on his face. Jimmy winks at me, as if to say, that's me told, but there's no animosity between them, and I can't help but wonder if they are good friends. And with that Jimmy shouts to Shadow,

"Come on lad let's get your stuff."

Shadow looks at Edward, as Edward says,

"Go on with Jimmy." And he happily follows him out slowly from the room as we both quietly laugh at each other.

"It's a good job you weren't wearing the basque bent over the sofa with me stroking and admiring that arse of yours, could you have imagined his face?"

"No, I certainly couldn't, but I could have imagined mine."

"Umm…me too!" he teases with a very dark wicked smile. My pulse races at the look he's giving me then as though nothing has happened, he shouts, "Come on were going to be late for your Grans."

"I'm well aware of that." I babble knowing he can take me from calm to nerves at any given moment. He winks, because he knows he has, then suggestively glances towards the Basque from Paris. I shake my head once again, putting on my new coat and pulling on the boots, as we make our way out through the door, collecting the Christmas gifts for Grans house.

We meet Jimmy in the hallway with Shadow and we all leave together, exchanging Merry Christmases, and I've got the most ridiculous smile on my face which doesn't want to leave. Jimmy heads off with Shadow to his lodge and we head of for my Grans.

Chapter 8

As I stand at the door before entering the lounge, drinking in this fabulous Christmas day and listening to Edward and William laughing at a program they're watching on telly. I feel loved, safe, secure and ever so happy. I go through the door to see William almost crying with laughter as I make my way around the sofa to sit beside Edward. My eyes flicker to the screen, remembering the program well and Grandad of course watching it and nearly collapsing in a fit of laughter. A laugh leaves my throat as I recall what's coming next.

'Muggers are about to snatch the councillors handbag, taunting her, the theme music starts, Batman approaches and the councillor looks stunned, the muggers scarper and Robin, shouts, "come on Del!" banging his fists together trying to look all masculine. Del-boy's eyes raise, the councillor looks bewildered, he nods and they both run off into the night. Edwards still laughing,

"Classic!" he almost shouts.

William agrees with a sputter and we all continue to laugh. Gran and Glenda follow into the lounge a few minutes later carrying a tray laden with drinks and goodies to eat and place them on the coffee table.

"Help yourselves." Gran says before sitting in her armchair next to the fire.

"The dinner Elizabeth, Glenda was delicious." Edward declares.

"I… it was Elizabeth, Glen, hats off to the two chefs." William adds rubbing his belly. Gran and Glenda both smile at them before saying in unison,

"Thank you."

I reach forward handing out the drinks then sit back and enjoy the rest of the Christmas special. Everyone's talking to each other when it's finished, and it's so nice to be sat in a room full of people I love.

I'm pondering on what Gran asked me earlier when we were clearing up in the kitchen. I'm not sure if I'm ready to take on the Baxter chains as she'd ask me to do. She'd said, 'she wanted to take a back seat after her seventieth Birthday and wanted me to take over the business in her place.' I was stunned at first saying,

"I knew nothing about the business." But that didn't faze her one bit.

'Nonsense.' she replied firmly, 'You know more than you think and I'm a good teacher, Abigail.' But it was the way she said, Abigail, sounding so confident and with so much determination that it made me think of how much she believed in me. I agreed to think about it and give her an answer on her birthday. I stare at Edward wondering what he'll make of the news when I tell him her intentions.

William's dozed off snoring. Glenda raises her eyebrows every now and again but doesn't say anything. Grans watching a period drama, Glenda comments every so often on how the other half live. This makes me smile a little, as we are the other half, but I suppose Glenda doesn't see us that way.

It's been such a magical day with my family. I'm staring at Edward who every now and again winks that cheeky wink, then smiles that wonderful, beautiful smile, and my heart has burst so many times today. Not just with the beautiful gifts I've received, or the fantastic Christmas dinner I've had, and not even the news gran sprang on me. It's my family that's made me feel this way, and Edward, because you can have all the money in the world and all the nice things in life, but without love they mean absolutely nothing.

The rooms got quite warm, and it's making me feel sleepy, so, I get up clearing the glasses. Edward gets up to help and gran just smiles at us both. I leave the lounge with the tray and start making my way down to the kitchen. Edward follows as I yawn.

"What time do you want to get off?"

"It's up to you Edward. I'll put these in the dish washer then have we to make tracks."

"If you like, I don't mind, but you do seem a little tired." I nod while filling the dishwasher, his arms come around me, then a kiss to the side of my neck. "It's been nice today, Abbie; you have a wonderful family."

"Thank you, Edward, I do, don't I." I reply pleased. "My grans a little bit of a dark horse though." He looks puzzled. "She asked me something tonight which took me by total surprise."

"What?"

"She said she wanted to take things easy in the New Year and asked me to take over the businesses in her place."

"And what did you say?"

"I was taken aback, saying, I didn't think I could. Which she replied, 'nonsense, that I knew more than I thought.' He nods. "What you think so too?"

"Abbie, I think you could do absolutely anything you wanted to do, if you set your mind to it."

"Really?"

"Yes, really." He grins. "You made me fall in love with you." I laugh hitting his arm.

"Shut up, you couldn't resist me - and your drunk." "Maybe I am, but I still love you." He wink's - I smile. It's quite funny seeing Edward drunk. I've never seen him drunk before. I've seen him tipsy, although I'm not in the least bit surprised, he's bladdered, seeing that William has been plying him with alcohol all afternoon and the champagne we had to toast our Merry Christmas. I'm surprised he can walk. He growls into my ear sending a cascade of goosebumps around my body. He cups my bottom with a firm hand lifting me slight and pressing hard against me. I blush, why, because I'm in my gran's kitchen with them only meters away.

"Behave Edward." He shakes his head.

"No... I don't want to behave." His reply is firm as he continues to squeeze my bottom. I raise my eyes, "You can raise your eyes all you want, Abbie, but you're mine, and God I want to..." the door opens to the kitchen and I nearly collapse on the floor, thanking God he stopped before reaching the end of that sentence. He smirks at me. I glare at him, knowing how bloody well he plays me as Gran begins to speak,

"You two love birds at it again." I laugh nervously as Edward rolls his eyes discreetly, and I'm thanking God again he didn't finish the end of his sentence as that would have been embarrassing. I walk over to Gran and hug her.

"Gran we're going to be making tracks now, we've an early start in the morning."

"Oh... okay. It was so nice having you both here today, you've made my Christmas."

"And you mine." I add with one last squeeze.

All our goodbyes are done and nearly half an hour later when Edward has decided to get in the car and put on his seat belt, we head back towards home. It's exceedingly hard trying to drive with a sex crazed surgeon sat at my side, who is making suggestive remarks as to what he's going to do to me when he gets me home. The basque from Paris has been dropped into the conversation several times. I've told him to stop as I was struggling to concentrate, because some of his remarks are very graphic. But he laughs and continues. I suppose he thinks he's funny, me-mowing my words back at me.

"I'll stop the car if you carry on." This makes me want to laugh, but I don't as I know it will encourage him more. So, I huff, and puff instead muttering under my breath and try my very best to continue concentrating. He eventually stops as he knows I'm not biting, and stares with a very sultry look on his face, which I think is even worse, since I know exactly what he's thinking. My heart's racing so much as I pull through the gates heading up towards the house. The Beast comes to a gradual stop as I applied the brakes. His seat belt comes off quickly,

"Get out of the car." he almost demands. I giggle. "You find this funny - woman?" he brawls. I nod.

"Oh – you do, do, you!" I squeal loudly almost making myself jump as he picks me up off my feet, practically throwing me over his shoulder then slaps my bottom. "I think I need to show you some manners Miss Baxter"

"Put me down."

"I will on the bed. Now shut up." He growls slapping me again. My pulse hits red, because the slap was nice a lot nicer than I thought it would be, and quite honestly, I'm very turned on. That very silly noise leaves my throat, one which I know Edward is attuned to… "You liked that didn't you?" I don't answer, he repeats louder, "You liked that didn't you?"

"Yes, I think I did." He doesn't answer with words but a gruff as he opens the door then kicks it shut with a foot. He's marching down the hallway with me still over his shoulder not speaking but breathing heavy. I'm almost shaking in anticipation at what he's going to do, but I'm not scared at the thought that he might spank me. I'm excited and he knows I am. He walks over to the bed and places me down.

"Take of your clothes." He commands sitting at the edge of the bed, his back straight and his legs together. And I do while he watches every single move I make. I'm naked stood in front of him, he's fully dressed staring at my body, then face. He beckons me towards him with a finger. I walk slowly towards him, my heart racing my pulse pulsating and every single nerve is on high alert. "I'm not going to hurt you." I nod. His eyes close in agreement. He takes my hand pulling me towards the side of his leg. "Bend over my knee." I stare, he nods. I move forward bending, my breast fall onto one of his legs, he inhales sharply as the rest of my upper body falls onto the other. I'm now leant across his knee, my feet on the floor, my head facing down. "Look at me." I turn my head towards him, his eyes have an erotic glaze which sends goosebumps spiralling through me. His hand gently caresses my bottom making me gasp. "Umm…" he breathes, slightly moving his hand closer towards my sex. I swallow down wanting him to touch me, but his hand returns to my bottom. "You know what I want Abbie, do you want it too?" without thinking I blurt out.

"Yes!" because I do. I want more. I want to experience this with Edward. And that is something I never thought I would ever want, but with him. I do.

"Then ask me."

His grip firms on my bottom and his erection pushes into my side. His hand circles gently, then a squeeze, my breathing is getting heavy as I'm more turned on. His hand moves again towards my sex where his fingers brush slightly over me.

"What do you want, Abbie?" My head's whizzing. I feel sort of dizzy and try to steady myself by grabbing his ankles.

"You!" He immediately rewards me by inserting a finger deep circling it and pushing firm, I squirm rotating my hips as the sensation begins to rise through my veins. His other hand suddenly comes down on my bottom but it's not hard, it sensual and It doesn't hurt, it feels nice. My eyes roll as the most exquisite tingle hits my body, then core. My head flies backwards as he inserts another finger pushing even deeper. He knows I'm orgasming. I'm almost screaming in sheer bliss as the tingles cascade around my body. Another light smack, my core tightens. And I'm lost in this extreme pleasure as he fingers me spanking my bottom. Words flow from my mouth, words I never dreamt I'd say, but I am saying them, as I'm in a complete and utter trance of sexual ecstasy.

"Come for me, Abbie."

I submit with the most powerful orgasm that leaves me panting, "Yes, I'm coming."

I'm pulled from his knee, my legs still shaking, my face scarlet, and my breathing erratic. He stands quickly nearly ripping his pants and boxers down. He grabs my waist pulling me towards him, then lifts me. "Put your legs around my waist, while I fuck you senseless."

My legs are around him, my hands around his neck. He holds his penis and sinks into me. I moan as he starts thrusting hard, walking toward the wall pinning me against it. He takes my mouth with passion; his hands cup my buttocks. I nod, and he does what he says. Fucking me senseless into the night.

We're still stood against the wall and he's breathing into the side of my neck, as his orgasm is ending. I'm not moving as I don't think I can. I'm cover from head to toe in sweat, panting and thinking, God that was amazing. He gently let's go of me and as my feet hit the floor I wobble, and he smiles that wicked but beautiful smile.

"That good, eh?" I nod. His trousers and boxers are still around his ankles and his shoes are still on. He grins as I look at them, "Classy or what!" he comments looking down also. I giggle.

"I need the bathroom."

"Can you walk?"

"Umm...just." He winks. "But I don't think you can, like that?"

"You'd be surprised Abbie, what I can do." I just nod my reply as I wobbly make it to the bathroom.

I return just as Edward is getting into bed naked. I go towards the draws to get a night dress.

"No. No nightdress. Get in." He says firmly as he moves the duvet back.

"You have to be kidding me." His head shakes.

"Like I said, you'll be surprised at what I can do." I get in at his side and he laughs. "That was only round one."

"And how many rounds do we have?"

"I'm not sure…I've not made my mind up yet."

"Do I get a say in the matter?"

"Ah…No."

"Your insatiable Edward Scott, and in fact, I don't think your human." He looks puzzled.

"Not Human?" I shake my head. "Well if I'm not Human. What am I?"

"I think you're a sex God."

"Really" he says with a proud grin. I nod to confirm, "Umm…Sex God, eh?"

"Yes, I think you've been sent down from heaven to punish me with mind blowing sex."

"Sex God. Mind blowing sex." He scratches his chin pondering on his next line. "Well, you might be on to me!" I squeal as he drags me on top of him. "Your extremely good for my ego, Abbie."

"Just saying it as it is."

"You enjoyed that didn't you?"

"It was amazing. Truly Amazing." He nods, liking my answer.

"Sleep, or round two?"

"Umm…I think round two" I say, seductively raising an eyebrow.

"You're insati…" I kiss him before he can finish his sentence as I know exactly what it's going to be.

We're both breathless again, flat on our backs. Edward speaks first.

"Round three." I giggle slightly still breathless,

"No. Sleep." He laughs as we cuddle each other falling asleep, absolutely, completely and utterly exhausted but, what a perfect end to our first perfect Christmas together, and honestly: One I will never-ever-forget as long as I live.

Chapter 9

I wake still enveloped by his arms gently draped around me, and even as he sleeps, I feel as though he's protecting me. And he had to ask that question yesterday, 'How, how had he done those things for me?' He genuinely has no idea what an unselfish lover or friend he is, or how he's taught me to love - by mending me. I move my head to gaze at his face. His lips release a slight restless breath as though he's whispering my name and it's tempting me to kiss them. I think he's waking, but his eyes remain closed masked by those thick dark lashes and he looks confident and in control even when he's asleep and it's hard to pull my gaze away. I love looking at him whether it's asleep or awake and I honestly think he gets more beautiful by the day.

I breathe out gently remembering last night and blush. I think my analysis of him was right, that he is a sex God, an Adonis sent down from heaven to punish me with mind blowing sex. I wasn't expecting to like what he did. But I did. I imagined spanking to be harsh, painful, domineering, but last night was far from any of those things. I stare wondering if he toned it down. But of course, he did, because it was nothing like the time before, even though I knew how turned on he was. It was more like a deep massage, not that I've had my bottom massage before.

I internally laugh wondering were all these thoughts are coming from. Then I wonder if he's spanked other woman, and if they enjoyed it, or did he enjoy spanking them, this makes me feel jealous immediately. So, I stop that thought straight away, because last night was all about me, him giving me pleasure, and an orgasm that took my breath away. But also, it was about trust. Me trusting him and me letting go. I grin to myself rolling my eye's thinking, well that's my take on it anyway, not that of course he's a little kinky, but honestly a little kink was good!

I'm wide awake, so, slowly I pull away getting out of bed. He breathes in as I've disturbed him, then slowly releases it into the air, which sounds like a tune playing calmly in my ears. I smile making my way to the draws to retrieve a night-dress, place it on, before heading off downstairs.

It seems funny as I hit the bottom step and Shadows not there to greet me. I head down the hall into the kitchen first putting the kettle on, then the radio, whilst making my coffee, leaving his un-brewed for now. The presenter is giving out facts for the meaning of Boxing day. He sums up with,

"So, that's why they call it Boxing day." I nod in agreement at what he's said, knowing I didn't know that either. A fab tune comes on which makes me immediately start humming out-loud and wiggling my slightly red bottom in time to the music. I feel so cheerful humming and tidying around the kitchen moving in time to the beat. I return the kettle to boil for his coffee, pour it out before making my way upstairs to shower. Edwards stirring as I place his cup on the bedside table.

"Morning." I smile with a bounce in my voice.

"Morning." He replies sleepily, stretching out his arms and legs before sitting up against the headboard. His lips release, "Thank you," but his body language is telling me something else as I gaze at his half naked body that's in view, then down towards the rest of him that's covered with a sheet, leaving nothing to my imagination. His eyes raise as he's noticed I've seen, but his stare continues watching my every move as I make my way around the room getting my clothes ready. I turn smiling back towards him, wondering, no, knowing that he's bewitched me.

"I'm going for a shower; would you like to join me." His grin is slow, as he seductively nods, yes. That very silly smile is still on my face as I enter through the dressing room, momentarily followed by Edward.

He walks back inside the hallway returning from the car, as he's been loading it with the presents, hamper and our overnight bags. I get a kiss to my lips which is chilly, and he smells of fresh air. He winks, "Are you ready?"

"Yes."

We leave the lane heading towards the motorway. "How longs the drive?"

"About an hour and a half, dependent on traffic."

"Oh, good, you can tell me all about your family on the way."

"Eh…do I have to?"

"Yes, you can give me the low down then I'm up to speed when I meet them." His eyes roll as if it's a chore him having to tell me.

"Hell, it'll take longer than an hour and a half to tell you about my family."

"Why?"

"There's loads of them."

"Well you better get started then." He breathes in but starts a little forced as he's talking like a robot, rhyming everyone off. He tuts as I ask. "So, who's married to your sister, Amelia." He starts again with a very exacerbated breath.

"I have two sisters, and one brother. Simon and Amelia are twin they're both thirty-one. My other sister, Emily, is your age, twenty-six. Amelia is married to John they have two children, Isabelle and Rosie."

"How old are they?" his eyes roll again, and I try not to laugh, "God Edward you have no patience what-so-ever." His eyes raise this time.

"Last time. Amelia is married to John and they have two children. Isabella age five and Rosie is a month old."

"Aww…"

"Are you going to let me finish, you do know the drive is only an hour and a half." He mutters.

I nod, knowing how bloody bossy he is. I'd hate to work for him. I try to imagine working for Edward and asking the same question twice. Hell, his team must just nod and agree to everything he says, but I'm not one of his team. So, I poke my tongue out at him.

"Please, sorry do carry on."

"Much obliged, Abigail." I want to giggle now, because I know I'm irritating him, as he's just called me Abigail, he only does that when he wants my full attention, or he's cross with me. But I can't resist today because I feel in a very silly but happy mood. Although Edward calls it annoying.

"Simon is married to Fiona. They have twin boys Henry and Joshua age five and Scarlet age seven. Keeping up?" he remarks sarcastically.

"Yes."

"Emily is not married, she's single. My mother is called Veronica and my father is called Kenneth. My grandfather on my father side is called Albert." My eyes raise remembering Edwards second name is Albert. "Yes, I'm called after him. My grandparents on my mother's side are Harriot and Lawrence. Anything else you want to know?"

"Yes. Just say it again. Who's married to Amelia?" My belly's nearly shaking as I try to contain laughter because of the expression on his face, although it soon changes as he remarks,

"What" in a very theatrical way and I stop.

"You deserved that, you bad tempered bugger." He just laughs. "A lot of family then for me to meet." I finish quietly with a grimace getting a little nervous.

"You'll be fine, Abbie, they'll love you, trust me, however you will get grilled I'm sure of that, especially from my mother and sisters." I raise my eyes, sitting back hoping he's right, that they will like me.

We head off the motorway down some country lanes. Before long he's indicating through an open gated drive, but you can't see any houses. I stare around the fields as we continue up the long road. I see the house coming into view but it's not a house it's an estate. My eyes widen as I stare at him then back towards the house. It's gigantic and appears to have hundreds of bedrooms.

"This is your parent's house, where you grew up?" He nods, and it's the same nod, one without airs or graces. "Gosh, you really where the playboy before I met you!"

"Umm… that's why they all want to meet you. The woman who tamed the playboy."

"Stop it Edward, be serious. I'm bloody petrified now." The Beast comes to a stop next to a bright red Ferrari. Along with an array of more expensive cars. "Seems like there all here. Ready to meet the Scott's, Abigail." Oh lord, I breathe but nod, yes, instead.

The door flies open as we're getting out, children start running down the steps, shouting with shrieks of delight. "Uncle Edward, uncle Edward!" his arms automatically open wide as he kneels to the floor and the children bombard him with hugs and kisses. I'm speechless watching. He looks a natural around children.

"Hey kids, meet, Abbie." He says to them nearly falling over. They wave at me.

"Hi Abbie." They all say together. One of the twin boy's shouts, "Uncle Edwards got a girl-friend." And they all burst out laughing, including Edward, who rags his hair,

"Off with you Henry, go and find your dad." They all giggle and run inside to fetch Simon. I can hear their excited voices,

"Dad, dad, uncle Simon, uncle Edwards here!" I smile at Edward who is returning to his feet and walking over to me.

"Well that's most of the little Scott's out of the way, just the big ones left."

"Hi, Abbie – Edward do you need a lift." Simon asks followed by another man. His hand comes out to me, I shake it as he introduces himself.

"Hi, I'm John."

"Abbie." I say shaking his hand, as Edward and Simon are getting our things from the boot. A beautiful stunning lady is approaching the car smiling at me, then Edward. I don't need any introduction, as I know this is Amelia. She's beautiful. Long dark hair, and the most beautiful blue eyes. They certainly have a way with them the Scott's holding your gaze with their eyes. Then I wonder where Edward gets his green eyes from. Another Scott appears it's Emily she's just as beautiful as Amelia with the same blue eyes.

"Hello" they both say nearly at the same time. Then Amelia takes the lead. "Please to meet you, Abbie, I've heard quite a bit about you, from Simon." She's interrupted by Emily.

"He's been giving us the low down on you." I stare quickly towards Edward who just raises his eyes at his sisters.

"I told you, Abbie, you'd get a grilling." He sniggers towards Emily.

"Nonsense, Edward" she laughs first before continuing, "We're all dying to meet the woman who has tamed our Playboy brother."

"Em...ily" he replies, in a very authoritative voice, as though he's telling her that's enough. She just laughs, threading her arm through mine escorting me indoors. Simon makes a comment, as I'm being led away.

"That's all your secrets gone now mate." He doesn't answer, but I can imagine his eyes rolling, as they're following us inside.

Fiona I've met before at the hospital. She greets me first, holding a beautiful baby girl in her arms. My heart automatically swells and behind her is the most adorable little girl with stunning green eyes, this must be Isabelle. She smiles, and I melt almost immediately. She's the face of an angel and is the spit of her mother Amelia. Although they all look like twins. Edward places the presents down and Isabella stares at him, he bends down, and she flies into his arms kissing him and hugging him tight, he stands nuzzling her neck, and she's wiggling and laughing in his arms, her laughter is infectious making everyone smile and laugh. I breathe in quickly closing my eyes with the image of my dream coming into focus. The man nuzzling our little boy and spinning him in his arms. My eyes open, my smile huge, as I watch him, now with all the children around him as if he's a magnet and their drawn to him. They love it just as much as him. I've never seen him so relaxed, so chilled, and so much full of love for these little Scott's surrounding him. And I know today is going to be full of new memories, memories that keep adding to my happy pile.

"Now come on, who's hogging my favourite grandson." Says a blustery firm voice carrying down the huge hallway. "Edward it's been too long." He hugs his gran, who in turn hugs him back and kisses him on the cheek. And by the expression on everyone's faces you can tell that he is her favourite, her eyes have turned to no one else's, her focus is just on him.

"Gran, this is Abigail." She turns and nods slightly towards me, but quickly returns her gaze to Edward then starts piloting him down the hall towards the back of the house. "You'll need to impress her a great deal for any affection." Emily whispers into my ear. I don't say anything getting the impression she's right. There all talking, and Edwards name is mentioned several times before they disappear through a doorway shortly followed by us. The rest of the Scott's are sat around the room. Edwards talking to them as I stand in the doorway a little apprehensive of entering.

"Abigail, please come in." I'm beckoned by his mother; his gran turns and looks at me. Edward walks back towards me taking my hand.

"Abbie, this is my mother." She's very attractive, same dark hair but loosely tied back, and she looks young, a lot younger than I thought given the ages of her children. About forty-five although she must be touching sixty. Her dress is nicely fitted over her slender petite body, a silk scarf is draped around her shoulders. I want to smile as I notice her slippers, there bright red with Christmas bells on. She smiles at me, as I've noticed, her eyes raise,

"Isabell insisted I wore them, my Christmas present from her." And at that moment I relax, she's human and the same as Edward with no airs or graces. But I'm not convinced about his gran. I'm sure she's giving me withering looks. His mother's eyes are blue as are his grans.

"Where's dad? And Grandad's?"

"Collecting and chopping wood for the fire, you know them and chopping wood." Edward smirks as though he knows a secret. "Yes, Edward I'm not stupid I know they're out there having a tipple." His face alters, knowing his mother's not stupid. He pulls my hand as he's now leaving the room for me to follow him. We enter out onto the back lawns that surround the grounds. We take a path along the side of the house and follow it down. I've not spoken yet as he's keen for me to meet everyone. I hear voices as we turn a corner.

"Quick someone's coming, put the flask away."

"Oh, I bet it's bloody Harriot, checking up on me." I hear a laugh,

"Don't be daft, their moving too quick, that's unless someone's put new batteries in the old bird."

"Dad." Then laughter erupts.

"God, Albert never suggest that one to her."

We turn another corner to see two very spritely gentlemen sitting on a large wooden bench watching a middle-aged handsome man wheedling an axe.

"Edward, my lad."

"Hey son, nice to see you."

"Edward" his dad says, putting down the axe and wiping his hands on a rag. He pats Edward on the shoulder and turns his eyes towards me, "And this must be Abigail." Edward nods as his dad shakes my hand. I look at him immediately noticing the green eyes, his dark hair and the same manly features. Edward is the spit of his father. I look towards the two grandads sitting on the bench with Edward in the middle, and I know without asking who Albert is, because of the green eyes. There enticing him with the flask, there like two naughty schoolboys. His father's head shakes.

"Oh, she won't mind, she looks like a nice kid." Say's Albert. I shrug my shoulders as though I'm saying, I'll leave it up to you. Edward smiles as his dad comments.

"Come on, we'd better get back, before you lead him astray again." Albert winks at me then takes me by surprise giving me a hug.

"Nice to meet you lass, I've heard endless tales about you." Edwards eyes raise towards me.

"Well move out the way Albert, because I know nothing about her." Lawrence adds taking my arm. "You can tell me all about yourself on the way back to the house."

"Leave the poor girl alone you two." His words are ignored by his father-in-law, "Edward, Ken, get the basket…while I woo this beauty." I turn to Edward who shrugs his shoulders leaving his grandad to guide me back to the house. We're walking in front, his arm threads mine, as he asks loads of questions, but he's kind and genuinely interested. We stop a couple of times while he gets his breath back in between questions. He's told me some stories about Edward as a young boy. The one about his teddy bear makes me smile. He lost it on a picnic, his grandad spent hours looking for it, but to no avail.

Edward cried himself to sleep whispering,

"Teddy gone." I turn to look at him in sympathy, his eyes meet mine with an inquisitive look. I want to hug him. I could imagine his sweet face, upset, little tears running down his cheeks for the loss of his teddy bear as we walk back to the house.

We enter the back through a porch where we remove our boots and coats. "Abbie, through there, down the corridor and the door at the top is into the kitchen, I'm just going to help grandad with his boots." Edward says.

I nod, before padding my way down the corridor in my bright stripy socks that sort of clash with my outfit. And to be perfectly honest they look a little bespoke with my skirt, but again I was not expecting to take my boots off and I suppose it's better than my bear feet, plus I don't know where Edwards put our bags, so, I can't retrieve any shoes. I enter through the door into the kitchen to a turn of heads, several people are cooking at a large Aga stove, talking and commenting on how long the bird will be. There not Scott's, helpers maybe? I get a flush, God, I think they have staff, then I hear that intrepid voice booming from the corner of the room.

"How, long?"

"About another hour," she huffs, "I'll inform my daughter. Who's brought this?" she asks pointing at the hamper.

"I did." I reply, courteously as I can.

"Oh, it's you…I thought for a minute you where one of the staff." She replies looking me up and down. I want to roll my eyes, but I don't, because it's Edwards gran, so I smile. Her eyes raise, and she mutters under her breath but of course loud enough for me to hear. "I bet Edward bought it." So, I let her think he did. "And how do you support yourself, or are you letting my grandson do that? I'm aware that you've moved in with him." She's really starting to get on my nerves, but luckily the nice Scott's come through the door just in the nick of time.

"Oh, you too getting to know each other." Edward says with a smirk. "And the hampers here you brought, Abbie. Fred, can you open it and take out the champagne."

"Sir." He replies with a nod. Oh, I was right they are staff. "Umm… nice choice if I might say so sir, Baxter's exclusive." Edward nods. She pipes up in a loud tone.

"My grandson has always had impeccable taste and is far too generous with his money." He stares at his gran, and then at me. I discreetly move my eyes, to ask him not to say anything. He looks puzzled. Albert and Lawrence both roll their eyes as we all move from the kitchen and into the dining room.

"Well everyone is back, so, let's take a seat at the table." His mother says. "Enjoy your wood chopping dears." She asks tongue in cheek; they grin before taking a seat. The children are sitting on a separate table altogether at the side of the large table. They giggle talking to each other and discussing the latest new toy, that father Christmas brought. There's seventeen of us in total. The door swings open followed by a woman and a man carrying champagne flutes, some are champagne with strawberries and some with orange, for the children.

"Mary there's not much champagne in those for the children." Amelia asks, she bends to Amelia's ear,

"No miss, there just orange juice." She smiles.

"Isabella, champagne," Henry giggles, as they all take a drink.

This is so nice, family together, children playing and getting on, a sleeping baby in a cradle, staff serving dinner. I smile internally wondering what Glenda would think off all this. These are the other half. It's like I'm a cast member from an exclusive period drama, but, yet again, as I stare at his gran sipping the champagne that I brought, knowing full well she thinks I should be in the kitchen. I suppose just like the chauffeur from the drama.

"Thank you, Abigail," Albert say, raising his glass to me in appreciation. I smile, and everyone apart from Harriot, says 'cheers', as we knock each other's glasses. Edward winks at me and she sees.

"So, what do you do, Abigail?" I want to poke my tongue out at her as she's blunt before beginning her interrogation, but I don't - I'm polite.

"I'm a student."

"Oh, a student of what?"

"Nursing."

"Nursing? Edward you're seeing a student nurse?" I squeeze his knee not to respond. Although he doesn't need to, because Emily does.

"Gran you're such a snob." She rolls her eyes. Edward doesn't look please, and she can tell. But she doesn't let up.

"So, how do you support yourself?"

"That's quite enough, Harriot." Lawrence says.

"But…" she stammers as he stares. "I was only inquiring." She moves her head as though not to be outdone by him as she continues to enquire all the way through the starter, the mains, and dessert. I excuse myself to the bathroom wondering if she does interrogation as a full-time occupation. I meet Frank on my return he's just leaving the dining room with a tray of plates.

"Okay, miss." I shrug, "Harriot getting to you?" I nod, he smiles again. "She's alright really, although she doesn't like new blood if you don't mind me saying so." I don't answer knowing I'd already figured that one out, but also, I suppose she's just like my gran looking out for her family, and honestly that's how it should always be. Frank goes on his way. I take a deep breath - my hand now on the doorknob and just as I'm about to enter, I stop in my tracks hearing raised voices.

"For God, sake, Edward tell her who she is…No offense Harriot, Lawrence, but you're giving me a bloody migraine."

"Dad," Kenneth remarks. I can't enter now, not even if I wanted too, which I don't. So, I stand there like a mute extra waiting in the wings for my que.

"Okay, I'll tell her if you're not going to, just saws I can have a little peace." Says Albert.

"I knew it, she's a charlatan?" Harriot almost squeals.

"Granny." Emily almost shouts shocked.

"Mother, let Edward speak."

"She gets embarrassed, she doesn't like people knowing who she is because of her past."

"I knew it. I said didn't I. She's poor. A gold digger. Oh, dear me the family fortune will be gone in a month." Edward raises his voice.

"No, she is not, she is the total opposite. Now stop."

"But…Edward." She splutters quite taken aback. I didn't want that to happen, him raising his voice at his gran, because of me. He breathes out, I think realising he's just raised his voice at her.

"Her family's exceedingly wealthy." Albert interrupts.

"Nonsense." she replies, fearless of Albert. There's a pause, and then a silence.

"I think you know her grandmother?" Albert say's in a tone that he knows is going to stump her. And I wonder does she know my Gran or is Albert just saying that?

"I very much doubt that." I stand there with my hand still on the doorknob wondering whether to go in or just wait.

"You've just drunk her Grandmother's champagne!"

"Edward brought that." There's another pause.

"Grandad tell us, who is she, who's her grandmother?" Emily asks breaking the silence.

"Grandad stop it now. I think you've had enough fun." Edward say's with a sigh, as Albert titters. And I'm wondering how Albert knows so much about me.

"I think her name is, oh…correct me Edward if I'm wrong."

"Oh, for goodness sake spit it out Albert." She barks, but he seems to be enjoying making her stew. Albert clears his throat before announcing,

"Abigail Baxter. Elizabeth Baxter's granddaughter?"

"No way." Emily shouts out louder than I think she intended too. My eyes roll knowing the cats-out-of-the-bag.

"I think that's what I said, Emily. What's up Harriot, cat got your tongue?" He almost sings his words.

There's a dry cough in the room, "You know her grandmother quite well don't you Harriot, aren't you part of her bridge team?" Lawrence remarks with a hint of sarcasm.

"Umm… Edward, why didn't you tell me she was one of the Baxter's?" she asks her voice a little cautious now. "You must apologise to her for me."

"No, gran, you can apologies to her, and I didn't think for one minute you would behave like you have done towards her, does it really matter if she's money or not." There's no comment, his chair moves.

I can hear him moving towards the door. I run backwards towards the stairs then turn quickly as though I've just come from upstairs. The door opens, and he strides towards me. His head shakes, "I know you heard what was said and you've not just come down the stairs."

"How?"

"Your face."

"It's fine. Honest. She's your gran, Edward, and I suppose just like my gran, she's looking out for you. She doesn't want you to get hurt. She might have said it the wrong way, but that's what she meant, I think her intentions are good." He smiles.

"God, she can be such a snob." I laugh quietly saying,

"And, Albert can be so naughty."

"God, families."

"Yeah, families, good aren't they."

"Do you always see the good in people?" I ponder on that question, because I never used to, but that's another talent Edward has graced upon me.

"I'm trying, and family, well…is family, and we'd be nothing without them."

"Come here, you beautiful, amazing specimen of a woman." I giggle as he hugs me and squeezes me tightly. "Do you fancy a trip around the grounds before it gets dark"

"Yes, I think I'd like that very much."

Chapter 10

We leave the house again through the back porch grabbing our coats and boots before heading outside.

"Are you alright?"

"Yes. Yes of course I am. How did your grandad know who I was?"

"I spoke to him about you when we first started seeing each other."

"Oh."

"He made me realise something, saying, 'don't give up on her, if you like her that much or love her, then make it work.' I put my hand in his, he smiles.

"So, when did you realise."

"It took a while for it to sink in. I'd not felt like this about anyone before and it frustrated me. I needed some impartial advice which I knew Grandad would give me. I was with him that night I received those photos of you with James and he knew how much you meant to me by my reaction. He told me, *just go to her lad and sort it out.'* Although honestly looking back I think I fell in love with you the first time I saw you. Then that day I picked you up from the floor, and you blushed I had this overwhelming desire to kiss you, and then..." he breaths out, "and neither of those desires have gone away they've just got stronger."

"Really." He nods.

"Can I ask you something."

"Off course."

"Kiss me." I'm satisfied with tender arms, a kiss, then a hug.

"So, did your Grandmother think I was going to run off with the family jewels?"

"Probably knowing Gran, she's a little on the dramatic side." I laugh. "But the ironic thing is the house, the money, isn't even hers. Yes, they are wealthy, but the main wealth is grandads."

"Your, grandad Lawrence?"

"No, grandad, Alberts."

"Really!" I say shocked, because he's so down to earth.

"Yes, all the money was made years back by my great - great grandfather."

"What did they do?"

"Shipping."

"Oh, is that why you know so much about the tides and things?"

"No, Abbie, a different type of shipping." He almost laughs.

"Are you taking the micky out of me Scott?" I ask with a raised eye.

"No!"

"Oh, so explain?"

"Shipping. Cargo, goods, things like that."

"Your pirates?" He's amused.

"umm... you could say that, so you better watch your step."

"But I thought Albert, was a surgeon?"

"Yes, that's right, he was."

"So, he didn't go into the family businesses then?"

"No, his parents where so proud of him when he became a doctor, and then a surgeon, they employed a manager to run the business when they retired. But everything was left to him. The money, business, estate and houses."

"Houses?"

"Yes, he owns Houses all over the world."

"Where?"

"Italy, Rome, America, Europe."

"Wow!"

"So, you didn't fancy it either?"

"Fancy it?"

"Going into the family business?"

"No...I like using my hands." He grins and he knows the innuendo isn't wasted on me.

"So, who runs it now?"

"Dad, and Emily is learning the ropes."

"Good for her." He smiles.

"Well I think that's enough family history for one day."

We've walked a fair way talking to each other and of course he did continue to explain about old money and how it's inherited. We've even confessed our secrets, which aren't really secrets, because we promised each other, that there would be no secrets.

Edward told me I made a noise when we made love just before I orgasamed, which I wasn't aware of, but he said it drove him crazy. I apologised for it and he answered 'don't' that was all. His phones in his hand with the flashlight on as it's gone dark. We're laughing and joking with each other. Edward keeps making silly noises trying to scare me. It's a little eerie. There's not much sound, just the wildlife foraging in the undergrowth, and the wind hitting the trees making the branches sway which sounds like whispering. I suddenly scream spooked by Edward shouting.

"What was that?" his grip tightens on my hand.

"Run," he shouts. I try, but he holds back, stopping me from moving, then he starts to laugh. My heart's nearly left my chest,

"You swine."

"Your face, Abbie."

"Not interested Edward, that was cruel." I stutter pushing him away.

"Are you not my friend anymore." His lip comes out, so I turn my back on him, but he grabs me from behind holding me firm and nuzzling at my neck. I huff. "Sorry, is there any way I can make it up to you?"

"Yes, take me back to the house with no more shocks." I try to sound convincingly annoyed but I'm struggling as he nuzzles then gently kisses the side of my neck. He's not playing fair; he knows I can't resist that.

"Do you not like being out here in the dark fields, with no one around for miles and miles?"

"Stop it." He laughs again. My imagination is now on overdrive. All sorts of things are flying around in my head…. Is there someone in the woods, who's behind that tree? "Edward just take me back."

"Are you scared?"

"Not really scared…" Although I am. "I just don't like being out in the dark."

"Sorry." He winks "I was only joking." I nod, as we start heading back. It's late when we get back to the house. Grandparents and children have gone to bed. We sit and relax having a drink with the rest of the family, chatting and Edward tells them I was scared out in the fields. Emily and Amelia back me up though, saying, how Simon and Edward used to scare them when they were children. Emily was just about to tell me more of Edwards antics, but he soon puts a stop to it.

"I think it's time for bed, Abbie." I nod being polite, saying night to everyone and thanking them for a lovely day. He kisses his mother's cheek and she stroke's the side of his face with affection.

"You and Abigail are in your bedroom, Edward." He nods, before saying night to the rest of his family and steering me hastily up the stairs.

"I've never had a woman in my bedroom at my parent's house before, or my own house for that matter."

"Really."

"First time, Abbie." He replies with a seductive wink. I shake my head and he frown's.

"What?"

"Like you said, 'your parent's house," his look is one of disbelief and his body language I need not interpret. The door is opened to his childhood bedroom then closed quietly. He grabs me like an over excited teenager pressing his lips firmly against mine, his hands swiftly moving around my body as he's trying to remove my clothes. I'm not altogether against the idea, but in his parent's house. I compose myself the best I can and whisper.

"No."

He growls, ignoring me, opening my blouse and lifting my breast from my bra, his hand is in my hair holding my head firm, as the other finds my exposed breast.

"You're not playing fair." I pant.

"I never do!" he murmurs as his lips move down my skin towards my breast, sucking and nipping at my nipples until there erect - my voice is forced to be silent, as he moves down my body, gliding his tongue. I can't deny him, as my skirt is hitched up over my hips, followed by my panties being rapidly removed down my thighs. He drops to his knees pressing his expert lips firm against my sex. I tug his hair, pulling in my lip hard. I want to scream and moan in appreciation, but I can't. My legs lifted at the knee and held to the side. I try to balance on one leg and keep my mouth closed as he takes me ravenously with his tongue and mouth.

I wobble steading myself holding onto his shoulders. God, my orgasms coming fast, he's generous and not stopping, my core burns on fire then knots taking my breath. I can hear the rest of the family coming along the landing retiring to their rooms as he holds me fast, and I'm hypnotised by my own desires. My body shakes with the breath-taking speed of my climax and he doesn't stop. I try feebly to push his head away, but he increases the pressure and slaps my bottom sending divine goosebumps all over that build then explode before fading like a prestigious fire work on my skin. My head swims with cravings for my own wants and needs as his family pass the door. I can almost hear them breathing. Oh, God the doors not locked - what if someone comes in, these thoughts are adding to my excitement, they shouldn't, but they are. He slaps my bottom again, and I erupt like Mount Vesuvius flinging my hand to my mouth trying to muffle the cry as I climax with such force nearly falling on top of him. I'm suddenly pulled to the floor; his mouth takes mine with passion and his tongue invades because he knows I'm going to let go. I try to catch my breath, as he moves to his knees spreading my legs wide. My head shakes, but to no avail. Two fingers invade me, rotating and pushing until my body bows and my back arches in compliance. He watches silently, my eyes roll. I need to scream, to moan, to release, but I can't - I must take what he's doing in silence. My legs are trembling with the force of the orgasm,

"Keep coming," his words instruct me, and his eyes make me obey. I grab at his hair forcing his mouth to mine where I take his lips hungrily to stifle my cries. The house sounds deadly silent apart from my ragged breathing. His eyes lock on mine and they crave my desire for him.

"I love watching you come." He whispers biting my bottom lip.

"Edward that was unfair."

"Why?"

"You know, why?"

"I don't?"

"Because we are here in your parent's house, and you know how I scream and moan. What if they'd have come into your room?"

"They wouldn't have done that, and anyway the door is locked."

"You locked the door?"

"Yes, of course I did. I just wanted you, Abbie, and when I get that urge that feeling nothing on this earth can stop it. And when you make that noise, that slight moan, your breathing changes it's intoxicating, and I can't stop, until you stop." I shake my head, because I don't know what else to say. "Do you need a hand getting up?" I nod, as he helps me to my feet. My blouse is undone, my breast exposed, my skirt around my hips and my knickers somewhere in the room. I roll my eyes at my stripy socks and he grins.

"Classy." I smile, knowing I looked like he did last night.

"I was going to say, sexy." My head shakes again and his tilts to the side, looking so cute. I wiggle my finger in front of his face.

"No more." I mime.

His lip comes out pouting and he looks even cuter. I remove the rest of my clothes and place the nightdress on I've brought with me. He's sulking holding up his pyjama bottoms. I nod, 'yes' and he puts them on remaining to sulk as we climb into bed. "Are we at least allowed to cuddle, Abbie?"

"Cuddling's fine, but no spaghetti arms." He sighs placing his arm around me.

I'm taken aback because that was a lot easier than I thought it was going to be. Hell, Edward has listened to me for once. But it doesn't last long. He pulls me on top of him quickly and holds me firm. I feel his erection immediately. My eyes roll.

"Now don't give me those eyes, Abbie, you know you can't resist me." He comments, flipping me onto my back. And it's true. I can't. No matter how hard I try, I just can't resist, Edward Scott.

Chapter 11

I wake early next morning, although I say morning as I'm not sure of the time, it must be before seven as it's still dark outside and the house is in silence. I turn facing my Adonis smiling and watching him sleep. I've a wicked thought in my mind and I know that is what has woken me in the first place. It's payback time. I smile wondering if he can stay silent, as I was forced to do last night.

I move my lips to his and gently kiss them once. Then slowly down his chin before moving onto his neck and chest laying small feather like pecks as I move towards his stomach and begin rolling my tongue followed by a kiss. He tenses slightly then relaxes. I glide my hand back over his rippled stomach not taking my eyes from his, before placing my fingertips gently onto his already erect penis. He's very consensual as I stroke slowly up and down watching his face. His eyes are locked on mine, as I whisper,

"I'm going to take you with my mouth."

I take him again and again as deep as I can, and he moans pulling at my hair pushing and guiding my head. He's just as greedy as me, wanting me to take him, but I move his hands to the side and look him in the eye as I continue. His eyes roll, his hands move impatiently towards my head, but I shake mine back at him telling him, 'no', and I see desire, I see wanting, before he exhales,

"Faster." But I stop, and I stare. His eyes close, so I continue, unhurried, at my pace, at my control. His hands grip the sheets, his body firms and tenses as I pick up speed. He thrusts his hips forward forcing himself deeper. I stop again - he stills - so again I continue. An impatient moan leaves his lips as he rolls his hips, and I know he's on the brink, but I'm making him wait. Beg, as he makes me do.

"Oh, God, Abbie," he breathes, as I roll my tongue over the tip. "Ple...ase." And it sounds so needy. So, I reward him moving quicker and he moans in pleasure. His hands are back in my hair, guiding me once again, but I can't stop him, not this time, because I'm turned on knowing what I'm doing is making him orgasm. I start tingling myself, taking him as deep as I can. He thrusts hard wanting more, his breathing is erratic, and his voice is almost a plea.

"Don't stop."

His hands are moving in my hair, pulling my head further guiding me to move faster. I run my tongue over the tip sending him into a frenzy of moans, "God I want to fuck you." His hands drag over my skin, he thrusts, his hips push and roll forcing his penis deeper into my mouth, nearly making me orgasm at his need to have me. I roll my tongue again over the tip tasting a salty liquid and it sends him over the edge. I lift my gaze to his. "Abbie, God I'm coming." I nod to agree, and his eyes close, he's biting his lip and he looks in total ecstasy. I take him deep and hard wanting this control I have over him, wanting him to come, to climax. His hands grip more firmly moving my head pushing me further onto him and I love this power change. His breathing is ragged as he moans my name. He tenses, thrusts hard before climaxing with force and filling my mouth with a warm salty liquid that hits the back of my throat forcing me to swallow quickly and pull away.

He's breathless climaxing on his back as I move back up his chest to reach his mouth, where he takes mine with vengeance kissing me hard.

I watch his face as he slowly calms, and he smiles that beautiful smile shaking his head, then he grins, "God, Abbie, that was amazing." I bow my head slightly and he looks more inquisitively at my face, because I think the pennies just dropped, that was pay back for last night. I grin in response exceedingly happy with myself. His arms swiftly embrace me, and I snuggle into his chest, my eyes close and as they do, I'm puzzled as he's not given any come back, although to be honest I'm to sleepy to comment and sleep takes us both.

We've been woken by someone knocking at the bedroom door.

"Yes." Edward answers to the knock.

"Breakfast is ready, dear."

"Thanks." He replies.

"Was that…?"

"Umm…yes. I think she's trying to make amends for yesterday. Come on shower and breakfast."

"She doesn't need to." I say getting out of bed.

Where both showered and dressed now making our way down to breakfast. I start walking towards the kitchen, but he stops me with a tug on my hand.

"In here, Abbie, this is the breakfast room." I lift my eyes and follow him in thinking, of course they'd have a breakfast room, silly me. We are immediately greeted warmly from everyone,

"Good morning - did you sleep well?"

"Yes, thank you." I reply to all who have asked. Harriot points to a seat next to her.

"Please, Abigail take this seat next to me, Edward can get you your breakfast." She nods at him as if she's saying, please. He smiles making his way towards a table laid with plates of delicious smelling foods.

"Sausage, Abbie, they look like your favourite, thick, pork sausage, umm… and there juicy" he remarks, poking one with a fork, and keeping a straight face. I cringe internally, and I know my face has just turn bright red.

"Uh…please" I say, but I know that came out all croaky. I smile weakly thinking; everyone knows what we've been up to this morning.

"Oh, are you getting a sore throat, dear." Harriot asks. I see Edwards shoulders move and I know darn-well his laughing at my expense. One more innuendo leaves his lips about sausages and I swear to God, I'll murder him.

He coughs, clearing his throat before speaking. I close my eyes briefly wondering what the bloody hell he's going to say. I knew this morning I shouldn't have taken him on, that his revenge would be sweet.

"She's fine gran. She's just probably got something stuck in her throat." My eyes widen at him, telling him to stop, that I was sorry, but he's loving this embarrassing me, his face has no sympathy at all. I mime,

"I'm going to kill you." He strides towards me with a plate of sausage, bacon, scrambled eggs, and tomatoes.

"Eat up dear, whilst its hot. Coffee?" His tone is straight knowing I can't retaliate. He bends slightly to my ear and whispers. "Now we're even." He pecks my cheek then returns to the counter for his own breakfast. I smile at Harriot who looks decidedly confused, but I'm convinced everyone else knows. She smiles, as I say, "Umm, this smells delicious." My face is scarlet.

"Oh, Abigail you look rather flushed are you coming down with something?"

"No – no, I'm fine honestly, it's just a little warm in here that's all." Edward sits at my other side with his breakfast.

"Umm…you do look flushed." He comments touching my face. My stare is one that makes him smirk as he's fully aware as to why I'm flushed. "Maybe you should take some more of that medicine you had this morning, for your throat." My coffee has nearly landed on Harriot's lap. I can't believe that sentence has just come out of his mouth.

"Oh, is it good. I could do with a good medicine for my throat, do you recommend it Edward." This is getting out-of- hand, I need to shut him up, before I choke or even worse land my breakfast on his Grans lap. My stare is deep at Edward, my eyes almost closed as a warning, 'enough is enough,' I clear my throat as he did and hope he takes the hint, as I look at his gran, but address him.

"I wouldn't bother with it Harriot, in fact it wasn't all that good…I'd definitely not do it again." her eyes raise, "sorry, I mean I'd not use it again." She nods with a little confused smile. But Edwards took the bait as his eyes have just raised and he's trying not to laugh. He winks then slightly bows his head in acceptance as to what I've just said. And we both start eating our breakfast and listen to

Harriot,

"Now, Abigail, I want to say I'm sorry about what I said yesterday." I shake my head. "Yes, I must. I behaved dreadful. But you have to be careful these days." I nod, thinking about Adam. "Remember, Edward." her voice lowers almost to a mime as if her next words are for our ears only. "Fiona and that, well…" he stares at his gran and she becomes silent. "But I suppose everything happens for a reason." I stare at her intrigued as to what she meant.

"Gran." Edward remarks with a discrete shake of his head.

"No…you're right." She replies quietly.

I'm now wondering what the hell is going on. He squeezes my knee, and I don't ask, and Harriot doesn't say either. We finish our breakfast and coffee's. The rest of the family left ages ago, some are packing, and the children are getting all their toys and presents together. Harriot retires to the lounge with a cup of tea to join the grandads.

I look at Edward puzzled. "Fiona was with a wrong lad some years ago when we were at uni. He was a nasty piece. That's how she met Simon."

"Through you." He nods. "That's what my gran meant that Fiona wouldn't have met Simon if the lad had been decent. Simon threatened him as he was in the police, a sergeant then. He managed to scare him off. It came out later he was after her money, so that he could carry on bumming his way through uni." I nod in agreement answering,

"Fate…doesn't matter who you are, there's just no escaping it."

"Well its fate that we pack our stuff and start heading back. Tom and Alison are due this evening, and Emily as asked if she can call later."

"No, I don't mind in the slightest."

"She also asked if we'd invited Jimmy for drinks."

"She knows, Jimmy? "

"Yes."

"Well then, we'd better ask him."

We're just getting into the car when Simon pulls back at Edwards arm, and slips something into his hand. I see this but I can't see what it is. Edward nods and Simon nods back, then I suddenly realise what the small thing is. Edward jumps into the driver's side.

"I forgot the keys." I stare at him and he knows that I know it was a fib. "Sorry." I stop him from continuing.

"It's fine. I know what it is, and I did say I wanted to watch it and prove it was him." He merely pats my knee, and no more is said about the small thing in his pocket until a few days later.

Chapter 12

It's the 30th December. Glenda and I have decided between us to do Gran's party on the New Year's Eve, so we can be there when she turns Seventy. This was down to a little devious preparation from Glenda, but when she explained it was to throw her off the scent as she really didn't want a party, I went along with it and helped her decorate the inside of the marquee with some personal touches. Now the small little venture has suddenly turned into the event of the year. Glenda was a little drunk Christmas eve, and seemed to have somehow invited most of the villagers to the party, and of course there's the staff from the deli's, the marketing teams, and the board of directors with their families. Oh, and not to forget her Bridge group which of course includes none other than Harriot, Edwards, Gran. Although I do think we put that 'little misunderstanding' as she called it, to bed. Glenda as asked Edward to invite his family as well. So, a small gathering of twenty or so people, which was meant to be New Year's Day has now turned into hundreds coming, well not really hundreds, but it feels like it, and you can imagine it's a day earlier and New Year's Eve. So, it's been none stop since then, arranging food, ordering a marquee which was very frustrating as it was the last minute. That task was left up to William, bless him, but as always, he came up trumps.

Remarking, 'Got a good deal.' It's heated, carpeted with an area for the dance floor, tables, chairs, lights. Food is being catered for by the staff at our local deli. When they heard of the party, they all volunteered. A bar is in place and Glenda has hired around fifteen staff.

We've loads of things to sort out today. I've to pick up my dress. Edward has some errands to run he said, but he was a little vague in what they were. I knew one was my new phone. So, were going into town together, doing our own thing, and meeting each other at the deli for lunch, then on to Grans to help Glenda.

Were up early and I'm waiting for Edward to get back from his run with Shadow. I've been stewing again this morning about the pen-drive, which to be honest I have all week. I'm not sure if I want to see it or not, I can't make my mind up. I glance outside into the garden whilst waiting for the kettle to boil. A little Robin has flown in and is sitting on the feeder. I smile, as it ruffles its feathers making him self-appear twice the size. I see another Robin nearby, and I wonder if it's, its mate. I watch as one flies away and the other appears on the feeder. Edward's back and calls from the hallway as Shadow bounds down to the kitchen.

"I'm just going for a shower, Abbie."

"Okay." I reply sitting at the table drinking my coffee, but my thoughts soon turn to the pen-drive. I nod internally, knowing what I need to do.

"Hi, did you enjoy your run." He nods taking a slurp of his coffee. "I've something to ask." He nods again waiting for me to say. "I think I want to see what's on the pen-drive."

"Now." I nod. His eyes raise, but he takes my hand never-the-less and leads me down the hallway to his office. I enter through the door behind him, then stare at him puzzled, thinking we've had the most wonderful Christmas and time off together, and do I want to tarnish it by watching that thing. He turns gesturing with his hand towards the chair for me to take a seat.

"Are you sure you want to do this. You want to do it now?" I lift my eyes not at all sure what I want to do. But then I feel a little surge inside, thinking, does he not want me to see it. Our eyes meet.

"But I need to see it."

"I know, Abbie, but now, timing, that's all I'm thinking about, you've a lot to do today and your meeting Glenda, remember, and there's your Grans party."

"But is there ever going to be a good time?"

"No. But what about tonight when we get back."

"Okay, yes, your right." I blow out deep and hard. "Well, as always, you're right, Edward." he smiles slightly, but doesn't comment, as we make our way from his office and out to the car.

We arrive back home and it's late. Edward did his errands in town, and I got my dress. We had lunch as planned then onto Grans to meet Glenda. Grans away for a few days and is back tomorrow morning or so she thinks. Her friend Agnes is going to delay her a little which I know will infuriate her pass no end, but it can't be helped. I'm just glad it's her doing the delaying, and not me. She hates being late for anything, as she thinks she's going for a meal with Agnes, Glenda and William. I'd made an excuse saying, I couldn't go New Year's Eve, but would be there for New Year's Day.

My new phone's set-up and Glenda has sent me some photos of the marquee now that it's finished. It looks magical. Gran is going to be so overwhelmed.

We're sat in the lounge. I'm fidgety, fiddling with my fingers. Edwards watching a documentary on the NHS, but I've not paid much attention, my mind is on the pen-drive. But it's also wondering again, and I'm scared that I'm thinking too much about it, and my focus is going backwards instead of forwards. I know what my problem is - I over think everything. It's hard not to, but I am trying my best not to. Although that's what Adam does, gets inside your head, spreading like an incurable disease. I turn looking at Edward, he's frowning at the man talking and not agreeing with him. He turns and winks. And I know he's my cure. My tablet to take away the disease. I wink back, and he smiles speaking,

"Come on let's do it." I stare now a little uncertain. "It's time Abbie, there's no point in sitting here all-night wondering what's on it, me wondering how you're going to feel and react." I nod, my response, knowing, he's right again, he's so rational and structured and so good for me. This is the second to the last nail in his coffin, just the divorce, then Adam out of my life for good. He takes my hand and as before leads me to his office. "Do you want me to stay?"

"Yes. Just put it in, and let's get this over with." I say quickly before I change my mind, knowing I don't want it looming over my thoughts any longer or I'm not going to enjoy Gran's birthday or the New Year. He inserts the little black stick into the side of his laptop. I almost hold my breath as the lights come on. Sound crackles from the speakers as it's loading. I take a seat at the desk. He leans over my shoulder guiding the mouse then hits play on the screen. Writing appears - Adult production - then loads of small print quickly scrolls the monitor. It goes blank, then the crackling sounds again.

I stare at the screen seeing a woman naked, her arms stretched way above her head, and she's strapped to a pole by her wrists that are suspended from the ceiling. Her eyes are darting around the dimly lit room. She pulls at the bar, but it swings backwards banging against the wall. I hear a door open and her eyes fly towards the sound, she pulls again at the restraints and the bar bangs louder this time. I can hear breathing as someone else has entered the room. Her eyes go wide as she sees them, her face looks scared. She pulls again at the restraints that are holding her fast, and the bar bangs once more against the wall, echoing in the empty silence.

A man walks over towards her, but you can't see him, only his back. He's wearing jeans, a black t shirt and a cap on his head. He drops something to the floor that makes a clanging noise, her eyes look towards it. The camera follows her body down towards her feet which have leather straps fastened on each ankle secured by two metal rings. Her stare returns to his. Her eyes close then open as if she's agreeing to something. He moves closer grabbing at her hair and pulling it tight saying something at the same time into her ear. He starts tapping her face on the side of her cheek,

She nods. He grabs her hair tighter this time forcing her head forward to his mouth and he seems to be whispering something again into her ear.

"Yes, sir." She answers, confidently.

His fingers run down her body, nipping and pulling at her skin until he reaches her nipple. He yanks and twists until she cries out. My eyes close, my hand reaches towards my forehead. Edwards hand touches my shoulder and he squeeze's gently but doesn't speak. I hear the bars rattle. I blow out reopening my eyes to see her head jolting back. He moves away, and her eyes follow him around the room. He walks back towards her, drawing back his hand before slapping her hard on the breasts. She cries out again and the bar bangs and the chain rattles with the force of the blow. He breathes deeply as though it's giving him pleasure. He's stood in front of her with a stance of arrogance, but you still can't see his face. His arm comes back, and I see his clenched fist move towards her. The camera is now pointing towards her stomach. I freeze staring at the screen. I don't want to watch, but I can't turn my head away. So, I stare in horror as if it's in slow motion. He hits her in the stomach, the bars rattle, the chains above swing as she gasps for breath winded by the punch. Her head falls onto her chest, he draws his fist back again, she screams, and he shouts.

"Silence!"

My eyes close. I hear him snigger, getting off on hurting her, hearing her in pain as she whimpers, and dark, dark memories are entering my head. My tongue runs over my teeth feeling the bridge in my mouth, a pain hits my own body as my hand reaches for my tummy, my hand on an empty shell that should have grown life, but he took that life. He took that life away from me, because he could, and he felt no remorse as he did it. I feel as though I'm stuck in suspended animation. I can hear what is going on, but I can also hear Adam in my head and it's as if the two scenarios are merging and clashing in my brain fighting each other until I can take no more.

"Stop, stop, turn it off, turn it off now."

I know it's him, his voice, the sound ringing in my ears and not stopping. I scream,

"Turn it off."

The monitor goes blank. My hands are trembling, and our room is now silent, and I know Edward is staring at me, that he saw my tongue run over my teeth, my hand on my empty tummy. I open my eyes and turn towards him,

"Can I have my old phone." His stare doesn't leave mine. "Can I have the phone" I repeat. His eyes close, I raise my voice, "Edward… can I have the phone." I remain firm, holding my hand out waiting.

He reaches into the top drawer of his desk removing the phone before handing it to me. I breathe in deeply, holding the phone in my shaking hand, but the shake has now turned to anger, and I blindly walk past him towards the door.

"Abbie." He says, placing a hand on my arm and his expression looks torn as if he feels my pain, but I shake my head ignoring his face, his words and walk through the door, and down the hallway. "Abbie" he calls again. But I don't know what to say. I can't describe how or what I feel. My head shakes, 'no' as I walk through it.

The cold air immediately hits me almost taking my breath away. I breathe in deeply holding it for a second before releasing it, and it leaves my lips like hot steam evaporating into the cold air. I start walking down the drive, then turn heading towards the barn. I need some space.

I walk through the small door at the side and make my way over to the bales of hay on the floor. It's cold and dimly lit, the horses are starting to move as I sit on one of the bales holding the phone in my hand not yet knowing what my intention is. I asked him for my phone because I wanted to ring Adam, to tell him what a sick perverted bastard he is, but now I'm not sure what I want to do. I hear Edward shouting me, then his voice to Shadow, "go and find Abbie." He's calling my name. I breathe deeply closing my eyes, wanting to shout, I'm here, but the images from the film bombard my mind stopping me. I start rambling,

"Sick, sick, bastard."

All these years that is what he's been doing. Hitting, beating, controlling woman for pleasure. I'm not sure how I feel but I'm angry with myself for being drawn into his world. A world of perverted depravity. The woman must have agreed. She did nod, move her eyes, he must have asked or said what he was going to do, and she answered, *'Yes sir'* In acknowledgement before he did anything.

My hearts raging with fury, hell-bent-fury. And him. And him. That's all my brain keeps repeating. I mutter again out loud.

"I want…I want." I stop, because I don't know what I want. My emotions are on red, right at the top of the scale, just waiting to tip over. I stare at the phone and scream. "Bastard. Sick, twisted, bastard."

My eyes open first hearing before seeing Shadow entering the barn. He barks once letting Edward know he's found me. He runs towards me and sits at my side, nudging me with his head, as though he's telling me to get up. Moments later Edward follows through the door; his head shakes gently seeing me like this, it's as if he knows what I'm thinking and going through.

"Hey…" he says softly walking towards me with his arms outstretched. I pull in my lip tight forcing the tears to stay, and not start. "Come on, give me the phone, Abbie." My brow furrows as I stare at him. His expression looks puzzled as he sees I've not rang. Are eyes are locked now on each other's as I hand him the phone, knowing I don't want it. I don't want to ring Adam. I want to kill him. He looks confused.

"He's dead to me."

"Abbie." I shake my head knowing by the look on his face what he's going to ask.

"Don't, don't ask that question, Edward."

"But…" I cut him dead,

"I said don't ask that question." He breathes out and doesn't ask. I don't want to recall what Adam has done. I'm mending. No. I've mended and I'm not returning to that part of my life. His eyes raise.

"Did you ring him?" I shake my head in response.

"And please don't ask me why, because I don't know." His smile is one of sympathy, but I don't know if I want sympathy, but he doesn't ask why. "Please will you give me five minutes; I want to clear my head." He nods, 'yes'.

"But please come inside."

He reaches for my hand, I take it and his fingers interlace mine, then lock, his grip is strong, telling me silently he's going nowhere, it's meaningful, and I get it. I squeeze back, he smiles gently leading me from the barn. He leads me back to the house; his hand doesn't leave mine not even to open or close the door as he leads me through into the lounge, Shadow sits at my side, he leaves the room still silent and I can hear him walking towards the kitchen. Shadow makes no attempt to follow him, and Edward's not told him to stay with me. He pushes himself close to my leg. I stroke him behind the ear and his head falls onto my lap. I smile at him, then turn my head as Edward walks back through the door with two glasses.

"Brandy." He says, and I smile weakly, before answering.

"We've been here before."

"Then you know what to do." I nod this time holding my nose and drinking it straight down. His eyes raise. I blow-out. Shadows head raises from my lap and he stares at me, then Edward. I shake my head with a grimace at the taste.

"You, okay?" I nod standing up. "Abbie, I need to know…Did he do those things to you?" My heart jumps as I know I must tell him.

"No…he did worse!" His eyes raise in disbelief, because the beginning of the recording was bad enough, and I dread to think what was on the rest. But I think he's watched it with Simon, and I think this, because of the look on his face. He stammers,

"Worse!"

"Yes, worse. He took my life, my dignity, my babies from me, and nothing on this earth could be worse than that Edward." I almost sob.

"Don't let him win" I shake my head, because I've no intention of letting Adam win.

"I wanted to prove it Edward, that it was him."

"I know, Abbie, but let's do it together…and do it together for them."

Tears hit my eye's immediately; he pulls me quickly cradling me so tight to him that I almost stop breathing.

"But, yes, I'm okay." He stares watching my face uncertain I think of my reply, but I mean it. I am okay. Not that I liked what I saw, or the thought of my money paying for that, but what I do know, is that I want to hurt him, and hurt him badly. But I don't know how to do that. He smiles as though he can read my thoughts.

"We'll think off something, Abbie. And as I said, we'll do it together."

"Yes, of course, together… I mean that. I don't think I could have ever been strong enough to face this on my own."

"Well, you're not on your own…are you?" I look at him puzzled because that sounded a little like a warning. He stands, and I reach for his hand.

"No, I'm not on my own, and I get that. I promise, I'll do nothing without you knowing first."

"Good girl, because you know we'll have to be cleverer than him and one step ahead."

"Umm… but do you know what I think." His head raises waiting for me to continue. "I think we should discredit him."

"Meaning." I shrug my shoulders.

"I'd not got that far ahead yet." He smiles.

"Well two heads are better than one, or maybe three."

"Three…"

"Yes, Simon, I know he can be a little devious especially in his line of work."

"What do you mean devious? Bent."

"Bloody hell, Abbie, no not bent. Digging, finding stuff out, you know. How to get around things, legally."

"Ah, I see." I laugh. He smiles. "What?"

"That was nice to see." I wink at him, knowing I'm not giving up my life again. I'll not give up my smile, my laugh not for Adam, not in a million years.

"Another Brandy, Edward?"

"Oh… have you got the taste for it?"

"No, I still think it taste vile, but it does however seem to work." His eyes close in admission as I leave the room with the glasses for a re-fill and return with them full.

"Are you ready?" I ask pointing my head towards the open door then tilting it upwards. "We can finish these upstairs if you like." He nods, striding over, taking his glass, then my hand and leading me up the staircase. We enter the bedroom, he takes my glass placing it down, cups my face making me look into his eyes, he breathes. "I love you, Abbie, and I'll protect you no matter what."

I smile speechless as his arms envelope me and the grip is strong, its protective, and a feeling of security overwhelms me as I rest my head against his chest. I feel the bond, the closeness, his strength and he makes me feel safe, he always does, my Edward, my angel.

Chapter 13

I can't seem to stop smiling. Edward watches amused as the taxi pulls to a stop at the door.

"Cheers mate." He says, handing the driver the fee with a generous tip, and I know this because the drivers smile is now wider than mine. We enter the hallway were Shadow is waiting for us excited and dancing around. Edward pats his head as I continue to smile.

"Your very happy?"

"Yes. Yes, I am. It's been a night I'll ever forget. Grans face was priceless, and I know she said she didn't want a party, but for once in her life she was well and truly stumped, and I know I saw a tear." I blow out feeling emotional while kicking off my shoes.

"And how are your feet?"

"Sore."

"Umm…I'm not surprised you and Alison never stopped dancing all night, but it was nice to see you let your hair down." And it's true I did.

"I've had the most wonderful night, and another happy memory Edward to add to my ever-increasing pile." I get the raised eyebrows before he responds.

"Night cap…or bed?"

"Bed, I think. I'm shattered."

"You go up Abbie and I'll just sort Shadow out."

"Okay." I say with a yawn. He disappears down the hallway with the dog hot on his heels and I make my way upstairs still humming and feeling very happy.

I enter the dressing area, making my way to the ensuite. I can't seem to stop yawning. I use the loo, before I return to the dressing room, undress and put on my PJ's. I sit at the dressing table, removing my makeup and my mind wonders back to the party.

I'd spoken to everyone at the party, thanking them for coming, and I had to admit to myself I was the perfect host, and it felt nice to be involved and joining in, because before I would have hidden away, sat in a corner not wanting to draw attention to myself. I heard a few comments from some of the locals as I mingled around the room. *"There she is... I always thought she was a bit of a loner, but once she started talking, she didn't stop."* The other woman agreed, then made a comment also. *"Yes, I thought so too, but what a nice girl she is."*

I even plucked up the courage to say a few words for Gran. I was a little dubious at first but the encouragement I got from Edward made me do it. I found that once I started, I couldn't stop. It was easy talking about her and what a fabulous person she was, words just seem to roll of my tongue. I did however feel a little guilty as she smiled on at me, before I finished and gave her a hug and a kiss on the cheek whispering to her that, I loved her, and that's when I saw a tear. I know times like this are hard, Grandad, Dad or Mum not being there, and it hits you more on these special occasions. Loved ones who have passed on not sharing these memories with you, but Edward was a rock, and Glenda and William ensured Gran was okay.

Both Alison and I had some very keen attention from the local lads, although Edward was having none of it, and kept interrupting until I introduced him as my boyfriend, and when he was satisfied that they all knew I was spoken for, he nodded once and continued to mingle. That did make me giggle some-what, Edward Scott jealous.

Edward on the other hand was by no means left on his own. Oh, the attention he got from females made the attention I got insignificant in comparison. Every time I glanced over towards him there were crowds of woman stood listening, hanging on to every word he spoke. He winked when I caught his eye. I nodded and raised my eyebrows and he smiled knowing what I was thinking. But I trust him implicitly and that's a nice feeling to have. Everything was perfect. I don't think anything could top this night. The food, the music, the company. Dancing which I loved. Edward is a fantastic dancer. He danced with my Gran which for me was quite emotional and meant the world. And of course, Glenda and Mrs Bracewell had a turn around the floor with him, but he smiled all the way through. His family came, and everyone got on like a house on fire. Albert and Gran seemed to hit it off well, they spent quite some time talking and laughing with each other. Which was another beautiful thing to see, because I don't think I've seen her laugh like that, well not since Grandad died. Another surprise was Jimmy and Emily they seemed to be hitting it off very well too. A slow dance at the end and a kiss. My nose wiggles and I feel utterly content. I hear the door to the bedroom go and Edwards voice,

"Abbie, I've brought you a drink."

"Thank you. I'll be out in a minute."

"No rush."

I stare at myself in the mirror, knowing how much my life has changed. Edward fills my days, weeks, months with happiness and joy, and that is something I thought I would never have. I don't think I could be happier.

I enter back into the bedroom. Edward's sat on the bed, still dressed with a drink in his hand. He watches as I walk towards him and I notice he looks a little nervous for some reason.

"Are you alright?" I ask. He nods and pats the bed for me to sit next to him which I do. "What's the matter?"

"I've got something for you."

"Oh, yes." I say with a grin. Wondering what it is this time, as we are in the bedroom. "Another basque for me to wear…may be?" I answer tongue in cheek. His head shakes moving the object from behind his back and handing it to me to take.

"What's this?" I ask looking at a beautiful red velvet box now in my hand. His hand lingers on mine, he blows out a slight breath. "What's wrong?"

"It's a late Christmas present."

"Late. Why, what do you mean, you've already bought me far too much." His look seems serious which makes me stop and stare. "Edward?" I ask waiting for a reply.

"I've had it some time, but I couldn't seem to find the right time to give it to you, well that was until now, that is." I'm confused and intrigued at the same time. "I just hope it's okay and it doesn't upset you."

"Upset me, why would you think that?" His shoulders shrug, "You'd never upset me, but you are scaring me. What is it, may I open it?"

"Yes, of course."

The red velvet box is soft at my touch and closed with a gold clasp. I undo it opening the lid to read the lettering inside. *Bespoke: Forbes.* My eyes follow down to a red velvet cushion that fills the inside and laid in the centre is an open-work designed, heart-shaped locket, inset with diamonds that are twinkling in the light. I feel his eyes on me, as I lift mine to his, but I wonder why he thought I'd be upset.

"It's beautiful, Edward." His smile is nervous, as I remove the locket with its chain from the red cushion. His voice is soft.

"Open the locket." I nod, opening the delicate clip and one heart becomes two. My eyes widen seeing an engraved angel in each heart and tears immediately hit my eyes, my hand goes to my mouth, he whispers, "Turn it over." And I do with a trembling hand. It's inscribed and reads,

Abigail's two special angels.

My tears fall cascading down my cheeks, my heart races and my mind is flooded with emotion, he suddenly appears shocked at my reaction taking my hand before speaking,

"God, Abbie, I'm so sorry." My head automatically shakes, and I want to say, I'm happy, but I can't get any words to come from my mouth. I'm overwhelmed and practically sobbing. "I should never…" my words come, because I can't let him think I'm sad.

"No. God, no Edward, please don't…please don't say that, or think that." His eyes smile at me. "It's, it's perfect."

He takes the locket from my hand and closes it.

"May I put it on for you." I nod as he goes behind me. I lift my hair as he places the locket around my neck, then kisses the side of my cheek. The locket falls towards my heart and he whispers. "Now, they will always be close to your heart." My tears fall faster as I turn flinging my arms around him, hugging him so tight and sobbing into his chest. "Hey, sweetheart, it wasn't meant to make you cry." I nod silently, because words can't possibly describe how I feel. What this locket means to me. I feel at peace as if they're with me. I feel sort of whole again, and I don't understand why, but I don't want to understand why, because it's the most beautiful feeling in the world. I have my angels here with me next to my heart for all eternity, and the man I love is holding me in his arms. He holds me close, and I hold him back for I don't know how long, and he just lets me cry and sob holding me tight in silence.

We finally break away. I smile at him with my red puffy eyes, holding the locket in my hand close to my heart.

"I'll treasure this Edward for as long as I live." I murmur kissing it gently.

"A New Year – A new start." He whispers, and I nod.

"Yes, a New Year and a new start."

Chapter 14

The weeks are flying by and I'm more than settled into my new life. My old life, the past four years now seem so far away in the distance. I've come on leaps and bounds and I've regained my independence, and I'm so loving my life with Edward.

Edward is still as bossy and possessive, although that is the wrong word or phrase to use. His very caring, looks out for me. He's loving and kind and that is so different to being possessive, which I suppose given the history of you know who, it wouldn't come as a shock to anyone why he worries if I'm not home on time, or if I go out. I know he thinks Adam is still lurking around and to be honest given what's on the pen drive I can't blame Edward being as he is. I'm also the same though when he's home late from work wondering if something has happened. I just wish Simon could find something on him and then we could put all this to rest. We've heard nothing from him which is a little daunting as Mrs Bradshaw has served the divorce papers. In a mad capped world, I sometimes think that maybe he's accepted the fact that I'm no longer his property to command, and he's come to terms that our marriage is over. I snigger, thinking, we can dream as I pull the Beast to a gradual stop as close to the door as I possibly can. God, it's not stopped raining for days. *Raining, that's a joke,* I mutter as the drops bounce from the windscreen the size of golf balls. This is more like a tropical monsoon. But they have got it right I suppose this time on the weather forecast, predicting torrential storms over the weekend and most of next week.

So, I sit patiently waiting in anticipation for a little break in the weather, but of course it doesn't come. So, I know I'll have to make a dash for it as I remove the keys keeping them in my hand, before reaching for my bag and making a run for the door, but I'm not very successful in this tight skirt and the heels I'm wearing. I'm peed-wet-through by the time I reach the door flinging it open, only to see Shadow sat waiting for me.

"I hope Jimmy's taken you out" I say, hurling my bag on the ottoman, followed by kicking my shoes down the hall. He stares at me then turns and walks back towards the kitchen. It's as though he's sulking, he obviously thought it was Edward. I shout out to him before heading towards the stairs to change out of my wet things. "I miss him too." But of course, I get no answer, and this does make me chuckle, knowing I'm at it again, talking to the dog.

I'm now showered, warmer, and changed into my fleecy Pyjamas making my way to the lounge. Mobile in one hand and a steaming coffee in the other. I nudge the door

open with my foot and enter, a little, "umm…" of appreciation leaves my lips as I feel the warmth escape from the room, then hear the crackles of the logs burning in the inglenook, glowing making the large room cosy. I bless jimmy for lighting the fire knowing how thoughtful he is, before taking my place in the large comfortable chair, momentarily hypnotised by the dancing flames, but I'm soon distracted by Shadow entering huffing and puffing sounding like an old man that's just run a marathon, and he couldn't make it any clearer if he could talk that he was fed up. He plonks himself next to my feet staring at me as I make myself comfy. He lets out a yawn, watching me with his big brown puppy dog eyes. It makes me feel sort of sorry for him, so, I stroke his head as my tummy rumbles. I'm hungry. I glance at the clock, it's eight-thirty already. I'm home late again tonight but come to think of it I've not left the office or one of the delis before seven all week. I ponder on that thought waiting for Edward to ring. He did say he'd ring tonight about eight-ish, but he's also late, and as 'sure as eggs are eggs' as my gran would say, he'll ring just as I'm warming my tea, it's as though he's a camera on me.
I smile, knowing how proud I am of him. He's away in London filming no less. The trust had asked him if they could film his teaching seminars for the use as training

videos for students, doctors and registrars. He's becoming quite the celeb! And I can't wait to see them. My phone rings and I grab it excited to hear from him…

"Hello…you're late this evening?"

"I am, yes, sorry, we ran over."

"How is it going?"

"It's actually better than I thought it would be."

"Oh, good, I'm glad. I know you were a little nervous." I hear a tut. I grin waiting for his response, knowing what he's about to say.

"Me, nervous! Never."

"Okay, if you say so. Are you able to get back for the weekend?" silence for a second.

"Umm…that might be a problem."

"Why?"

"They've asked if they can film in theatres while they have the crew down here." I huff… "But I'll try."

"No, if they need you to film then I suppose you'll have to stay. So, you won't be able to make the night out on Friday then?"

"Night out, What night out?"

"Oh, yeah, sorry, I forgot to mention it. Alison has arranged for us to go out with your sister's and hubbies on Friday night to celebrate my new job, but it looks as if I'll have to play Gooseberry."

"This Friday?"

"Yes. You were meant to be back. Remember?"

"Where are you going?"

"I'm not sure, Alison's arranged it."

"I see…" his tone sounds not too pleased.

"What…you're not happy I'm going on my own?" no reply. "Or that I'm playing Gooseberry?" still, no reply. "Am I getting the silent treatment."

"Sorry. No Abbie, not the silent treatment at all it's just that I'll miss that too, and you're going to be on your own again."

"It can't be helped." He sighs disappointedly, but this however makes me smile again, knowing he meant that last comment. And to be perfectly honest I am disappointed, but I can't say, because this is a fantastic opportunity for him, and I also see it as a great honour.

"I was gutted that I wasn't there to support you on your first day."

"It's fine." I answer, but honestly, I was disappointed, but I never said so. The filming is too big of an opportunity for him to miss. I can almost see him smiling as he asks.

"So, how is your new job going?"

"It's good - yes, but tiring, and my feet are so sore. I've blisters on blisters and my pinkies are the size of my big toes." He laughs…

"Pinkies…. Don't you mean your little piggies are the size of your big toes." I know he's right as I remember the rhyme now, but it still doesn't stop me poking my tongue out. "Abbie are you sticking your tongue out at me?" Shit, he has got a camera on me, but I reply coyly.

"No… me never." He laughs, knowing I was. "Then sweetheart if your feet are that sore, I suggest you wear your trainers."

"Don't be daft…trainers with the Prada suit you bought me? I don't think so."

"Umm…" he murmurs… "That Prada suit. I got the picture you sent me. Very sexy indeed, Miss Baxter."

"Trust you. I thought I looked very sophisticated."

"You did, and extremely fuckable."

"Edward Scott" I splutter. He laughs, so I think I'll play him at his own game. "Would you like me to wear it for you when you get home, we could do a little roll play, if you like?"

His voice is suddenly serious. "Roll play…what do you have in mind?" he asks very slowly, and I love this, flirting with him.

"I thought maybe you could be the big shot surgeon and I could be your shy secretary." he breathes deeply, and I know he's imagining it. "Would you like that Mr Scott?" and for a second there's a silence.

"Abbie, you can stop that right now, if I start thinking or picturing that I will have to drive back home tonight." I giggle then continue with my seduction.

"Well, seeing that I'm playing Gooseberry on Friday I'll just have to wear the Prada suit then and see what I can pick up." He bats straight back all cocky and smug.

"Abbie… you can't even pick up your purse when you drop it, let alone another bloke. You're too besotted with me." He laughs, and I suppose he thinks he's funny with his comeback.

"Really, Edward, is that what you think?"

"NO. That is what I know." His remark is so conceited as if he's the bees- knees - which of course he is- but I'm definitely not letting him get away with that.

"Well, we will just have to see about that then, won't we." But Edward being Edward doesn't bite the arrogant sod. So, I carry on not wanting him to get the better of me, so, I'm going to make him squirm.

"Umm…I've just finished work. Gosh it's warm. My fingertips slide to the buttons of my blouse opening them slowly to my cleavage. My short skirt clings to my warm thighs just enough to show the outline of my suspender belt and lace-top stockings. I'm sat at the bar tossing my hair around trying to cool myself down while sucking on an ice cube that drips down my lips falling onto my half-exposed breast." He shouts. I squeal and laugh triumphant in my quest, knowing I've got to him, because by now I know which buttons to press.

"You win. Fuck, Abbie, you can wear a onesie Friday." Then he chuckles at his loss.

"Edward, your language is very choice tonight."

"Then stop teasing me on the phone."

"Oh, but I like teasing you Edward."

"Listen you be careful on Friday. Make sure you get a taxi there and back and not on your own."

"Yeah, yeah…"

"Hey, I mean it." And I can tell he does.

"Sorry. I know. And I will." We chat for a little longer. My tummy rumbles again. We say good night, and he makes me promise that I ring him when I've returned home on Friday night which I must, because he won't hang up until I do.

I head off back to the kitchen and warm the tea Yvonne has very kindly left for me in the fridge. It smells delicious as it warms, extra garlic too, my mouth is nearly watering. I grab a glass and fill it with cold water in anticipation of the chili being a little hot before returning to the lounge and sitting back in the chair and tucking in. I was right it is a little spicy, but very good. As I'm eating, I have a little thought. I wonder what he'd think if I did. I take my phone and ring Alison. She answers:

"Hi, are you okay?"

"Umm…I just wanted to ask your advice on something?"

"Oh…what?" she sounds intrigued.

"Do you think we could put off going out this Friday?"

"I don't see why not…but why?"

"Well, I've just spoke with Edward, and he's staying longer in London filming and won't be able to make it back, and to be honest he sounded really gutted."

"Yes, that's fine, are you thinking we can re-arrange it for next week instead?"

"Yes,"

"No, problem."

"Brill, I'll message his sisters and tell them."

"Is that the advice you wanted to ask?"

"No, not really, but I've had an idea."

"Go on then, stop keeping me in suspense."

"Well I thought I might just have a little trip to London." She laughs, "you know to cheer him up." I don't tell her about the conversation I've just had about the Prada suit, but it has given me an idea.

"What are you up to? Oh, please tell." But this time I laugh because I've not yet worked out all the details myself, and I need to ask Gran for the Friday and Monday off. "You're not going to tell me are you." I shake my head. We continue talking and Alison asks about the job and I tell her. I ask her about the ward and sister, so she gives me the low down on everything that's been happening, and I do sort of miss it in a way, but the jobs could not be more different, and I'm loving working with Gran. I yawn followed by Alison yawning and we both agree that we're shattered. We say our goodbyes and arrange to meet for coffees at the deli on Wednesday.

I take my dish and glass to the kitchen and wash them before heading off to bed. I spoke with Gran asking her if I could have the Friday and Monday off. She said, 'yes' and didn't even ask at first, why, apart from, 'was I okay, and was I enjoying the Job.' Which of course I am, and she was thrilled that I was surprising Edward. She really does like him. After we ended our conversation I went straight onto the net and booked my train ticket. I wanted to fly but with the weather forecast I thought it best not to. My room at his hotel is also booked. I didn't want to risk staff slipping up if I tried to arrange staying in the same room as Edward or really explaining the nature of my visit. It did however cross my mind that it will be empty and a waste of money, but I suppose I am allowed every now and again to be a little frivolous and it's a good cause.

I wake early. Gosh this week has flown by, and I have felt a little guilty of late asking for time off so soon, but I've certainly made up for the hours and time lost. I don't think I've got home before eight most nights - showered then straight to bed. Edwards not pleased about the hours I've been putting in, but he doesn't know what I've in store and planned for the weekend.

Alison was funny on Wednesday when we met in the deli. She kept commenting that I was a high-flying executive now and would not want to mingle with students. Which of course I teased her about. She was like a dog with a bone trying her best to find out what I was up too at the weekend. And I must admit it took some going for me not to tell her and keep all the arrangements to myself, but I couldn't risk her telling Tom. Which of course she said she wouldn't, but if their anything like Edward and me at telling each other everything, then of course she'd have told him.

My little case is packed and I'm waiting for the taxi. I've dressed smart but casual for the train journey down. Jimmy has got his instructions for Shadow, and I've warned him several times I'll crown him if he slips up and tells Edward, knowing I had no choice in telling him the plans because of the dog. He's had me on pins all week and loved teasing me but to be fair I don't know how many times I've nearly slipped up when speaking to Edward on the phone.

I'm rubbish at keeping secrets.

A horn pip's that I faintly hear, then the buzzer for the gates. I press the button letting the driver through and up the drive. I walk outside to gale-force-winds, lock the door, and I've an almighty but nervous grin on my face, because it's time to let the games begin.

Chapter 15

My cab pulls to a stop in an allocated drop off. The hotel appears grand, as I pay the driver his fare before smiling towards a cheerful man asking,

"Any bags miss?" I nod getting out and he walks towards the back of the cab to retrieve my little case. "This way Miss." He gestures pointing towards the open door. I follow behind into the smart lobby area and make my way towards the desk as he places it next to me then smiles. I smile back going into my pocket to retrieve a tip before placing it in his hand. He nods and walks back to his post next to the door, waiting for his next arrival.

"A nice journey down, miss?"

"Yes, thank you." Although I know that was a fib. It was okay but crowded and I stood for most of the time as I gave my paid seat to a lady with a little girl, but all-in-all it wasn't too bad, three hours from start to finish. I glance at the time, two-thirty in the afternoon. I breathe out unexpectedly feeling nervous.

"Miss, would you like your bag taking to your room?"

"No, I'm fine thank you." I reply as I've only the one small case.

"Would you just like to sign in then please so I may give you your key-card." She asks sliding a form and pen over to me. I sign the form, sliding it back, and she hands me the card, commenting, "Floor Ten, room 1025, your room has a nice view of Tower Bridge, if you'd like to take the lift madam it's just there." And she points in the direction of the lift with a very beautiful manicured finger. I thank her heading off towards it.

I open the door to my room it's nice, large with a gigantic King size bed. A full glass window dominates the entire width of the room. And wow what a fantastic view of the city. I feel like Mary Poppins looking over roof tops towards Tower Bridge and the Shard. I'm not sure how Edward wangled this one staying at the Hilton, no wonder he said 'yes' to another film shoot. And I know, as he told me, the film crew were impressed also that he'd wangled it for them too. It must be costing the film company a fortune. I start removing my clothes from the case, hanging the Prada suit with silk blouse on the door of the wardrobe then my killer black heels on the floor. I giggle a little placing my basque and stocking with the thong on the bed before heading into the bathroom to run a bath. I start the bath running adding a few drops of the Chanel bath oil Edward bought for me. The room fills with the most alluring sent. Which again makes me smile with memories as I return to the room and telephone down to reception ordering room service. I order, a coffee, sandwich and treat myself to their delicious Lemon

Drizzle cake, it made my mouth water when I read the description on the menu. I didn't eat on the train, and to be honest I'm not at all sure what time Edward is going to be back tonight. I must ring him shortly. The baths filled so I jump in and chill. I've an hour to kill before my food arrives. I can't seem to stop smiling or laughing out-loud to myself. I feel daft but happy as I wonder what his reaction will be.

I'm planning to be sat at the bar when he arrives back from the filming. How I'm going to get him to the bar is another question I keep asking myself, although he has said several times they meet in the bar before going to dinner. I remember saying. 'it's alright for some I'm eating meals out of the fridge warmed in the microwave from Yvonne.' which I wasn't complaining about. But he did go on and on about the food being exquisite and four courses – to which I replied, 'he'd come back fat.' He laughed saying,

'May be, but I'll work it off in a couple of days fucking you in our bedroom.' I shake my head as I remember the remark knowing how blunt, but honest he is. I'm finally ready and heading towards the lift. I've done my hair sort of up but falling down, the wind swept look I call it. Not too much make-up. My blouse for now is fastened which I plan on undoing a few more buttons a little later when I see him, but before he sees me. My bottom wiggles so much in these heels and the tightness of the pencil skirt is adding to it. I've chosen the Black Prada suit today the one I sent him the photo of me in. The skirt is a little longer on this one and sits just below my knee, as I think my aim is to seduce Edward and not all the men in the bar. I enter the lift and press lobby. I glance at myself in the full-length mirror. My waist is small, my legs long and my face almost scarlet as I feel rather naughty wearing the basque underneath with the lace top stockings. The lift stops, I enter the lobby and my heels sink slightly into the deep plush pile of the carpet. I get a sideways glance and nod from the man on reception, as I walk past followed by a comment, "Good evening, Madam, may I help you." I shake my head politely walking in the direction of the bar. I enter and glance at the clock, it's now Five-Fifteen and Edward said he'd be done about Five-thirty when I spoke with him earlier. It's surprisingly busy. A few people are ordering drinks, but most are sat around in the opulent seating area. It's quite noisy, people laughing and talking, and pleasant music plays in the background. I stare at the bar stools which are exceedingly high, and I try to work out a strategy in my head before attempting to sit on one. May be these killer heels and Prada suit were not such a good idea after all, especially when my aim is to seduce Edward, it may all end in tears. I wait for a lull at the bar, the tender turns to me… I order a Gin and Tonic knowing he must turn his back on me to get if from the optic.

Once he's turned and no one is in view I take my chance with the ninety-foot stool. One foot on the metal rim, not too bad, but now I've to negotiate my second foot which appears a little trickier, my hand I place on the bar as I lift myself up on the rim, but as I place my other foot on the shiny metallic rim it slips. I stumble forward but somehow my bottom lands sideways on and my skirt ruffles up, so I adjust it quickly before anyone sees but slide on the leather nearly falling back off before headbutting the bar. I'm convinced someone has polished the bloody leather. Shocked and momentarily dazed I sit straight trying to look sophisticated but poorly. The bar man turns with my drink and a wide grin. I stare at his face and notice I'm facing a large mirror. I nod politely knowing he's seen all. He nods seeing my embarrassment then comments,

"They get everyone!" I smile taking a large gulp of my Gin before he goes off to serve a noisy group of men who have just entered the bar which I can see through the mirror I'm facing.

"What are you all having?" A man asks the others who are following behind and just as noisy.

"A beer" most reply. The chap asking moves his eyes towards the lobby, Edward?" My heart jumps as I see him in the mirror, but he can't see me, my backs facing him and for some strange reason my hands begin to shake and I've to put my drink down before I spill it.

"Just got to make a phone call first. I'll order when I come down." My eyes rise upwards, great he's disappearing now. No, he's not, oh, he has. A few minutes later my phone rings. I retrieve it from my bag that I plonked on the bar, knowing I'm his phone call.

"Hi, how are you?"

"I'm good! and you?"

"Fine sweetheart."

"Drink, love?" I'm asked by one of the men at the bar, but not only one of the men, one that's with Edward. I turn my head shaking no, as my response, but Edward is straight on it.

"Are you out already?" I nod, because the chap is now walking towards me, this is just great stuff especially when Edward is on the phone. I'm hoping he doesn't, but he does. "Want a drink, love?"

"Tell him to piss off your spoken for." Oh, Lordy this is going to be some seduction. I don't know what to do. So, I panic and hang up, then turn to the chap answering,

"No, thank you, I'm waiting for someone." My phone rings again. God, its him and thank goodness the man walks back to the others saying something and they turn and stare in my direction.

"Your phones ringing, Miss." The bar man says.

"I know." I reply stuck in the situation and not wanting to give myself away. I swipe the screen almost cringing, to a reply from him that's not at all impressed.

"Did you hang up on me?" Think, Abbie, come on...

"God, no I'd never." I raise my eyes. "I...I caught the phone..." I lower my voice before continuing, "as I was telling that chap to piss off like you asked me too." There's a long pause, then he takes a deep breath and I'm hoping he's swallowed it.

"Is Simon there?" oh, bugger what do I say to that.

"N...o - I'm waiting for everyone to arrive, I finished work early so I came straight to the bar." He stops me dead.

"You're out on your own - sat at a bar?" I nod, but of course he can't see me doing this, but I can also tell he's more than annoyed. "Why are you out on your own?" I want to say, 'I'm not out on my own or waiting for the others. I'm sat in your hotel bar waiting for you to get off the bloody phone and come down to the bar so that I can seduce you, you Muppet.' but of course I can't say that, and I don't.

"Because by the time I'd got home from work I would have had to turn straight back around to come back into town to meet everyone." Silence again and I know he's not at all happy. "Do you not trust me Edward?"

"Of course, I trust you, Abbie. I just don't trust other men."

"I can look after myself you know"

"Umm…" and I know he thinks I can't.

"Anyway, I need to go now."

"Really…" His tone is not at all impressed again.

"Yes, sorry I'll ring you when I get back home tonight as I promised I would…" I press end because I know he's going to go ballistic at me. A few seconds later my phone rings again, then stops, then rings and rings again. The bar man just glances at it on the bar, as I give him a little weak smile to indicate I know its ringing, but no further eye contact is made with him just the bottom of my glass as I neck the Gin for Dutch courage. I'm now sweaty and fidgety and hoping to God, that he does come down to the bar. I'm not disappointed as he enters the bar a few minutes later, his phone is in his hand and he looks increasingly irritated.

"Edward mate, do you want a drink?" the chap asks who asked me. He walks past him and towards the bar. My backs to him but I can see him through the mirror… he catches the bar tenders' eye…

"Double JD on the rocks." Oh, God, he is annoyed. He drinks it straight down. "Another." He swipes the screen on his phone and presses, and I know it's me he's calling. My phone rings… but he doesn't pay attention at first. What do I do, do I answer or not? I take a deep breath staring at him in the mirror and I can see the frustration in his face as I've not answered. Okay, Abbie, answer.

"Did you hang up on me." His voice is cross, and he's not bothered who is listening or watching.

"Yes" I reply. He looks fuming, but I can't stop there. "So, what if I did, what are you going to do about it?"

"What." He shouts, and I see the others stop and glare at him, the bar man is staring at me. I shake my head as I turn in my seat hanging up on him again, and my God he nearly drops his phone in temper. He's still no idea I'm sat at the other end of the bar. I clear my throat and speak clearly and loud enough so that he'll hear me.

"I said, what are you going to do about it?" he looks up and puzzled, glances around the room then spots me smiling at him. His eyes are nearly popping out of his head, and he's shaking it with a grin walking towards me. He reaches me still smiling, and I know I'm forgiven, because he looks so pleased to see me. He breathes deep before grabbing my waist and leaning forward whispering into my ear.

"I'll tell you what I 'm going to do about it, and that is, spank the arse off you."

"Really!" I answer.

"God, yes." A tingle runs down my spine as he moves back almost undressing me with his eyes as I'm still sat on the stool.

"Nice surprise then." He nods favourably.

"You, naughty, naughty little minx." He replies slowly.

I giggle flirtishly with my reply "I try my best!"

"I need to get you up those stairs and into my bedroom." He murmurs into the side of my neck.

"Are you not hungry?"

"Umm…but what I want to eat they don't serve in the dining room." I cough politely.

"Really." He winks. "Well you'd better help me off this bar stool then, Edward." His hands go under my arms as he lifts me from the stool, holding me tight to him before placing me down on the floor. I smile, and his look is sultry. My eyes raise feeling him against me. "Well it does appear that you are hungry," he grins as my comment hasn't gone unnoticed before he speaks.

"I've missed you!"

"Me too!" I answer as he escorts me from the bar and towards the lifts. Edward holds back as the same man who asked me if I wanted a drink speaks to him as he's entering the dining room.

"Edward are you not eating with us tonight.?" his head shakes. No. the man nods before staring at me, which suddenly makes me feel like Edwards just picked me up in the bar and is escorting me to his room. Which of course he is, but not in the way the man is thinking. Does he think I'm a prostitute? Edwards quick to respond to the man's comment and actions.

"This is my girlfriend, Abbie." He nods with a smile towards me, as if he knows all about me, who Abbie is, which makes me feel nice, knowing Edward has spoken about me to his friends.

"See you in the morning then." He says with a wink.

"Yes, bright and early, as I now want to leave early tomorrow and show my girl the sights."

"No prob's mates. I'll tell the others." He heads off into the dining room and we enter the lift. Were alone the doors close and I'm just about to ask him, but he answers for me. "Yes, I talk about you all the time." I lean forward kissing his cheek.

"Thank you." He winks and turns me to face him. His arms squeeze the life out of me as his lips connect with mine and passion is not the word to describe the heat that is soaring between us.

The door opens to Edwards floor. Floor twelve. He immediately takes my hand almost pulling me from the lift. His stride is long and I'm practically running,

"Stop, Edward, please. I can't move so fast in this skirt or heels." He stops and turns as I'm behind him, but his grip remains firm in my hand.

"You can't?" My head shakes my response. I'm suddenly picked from my feet and thrown over his shoulder. His arm is tight around my legs on his chest and I can't move.

"Put me down." He strides down the corridor ignoring me, and I can almost see the grin on his face. I hit his back. "Edward Scott put me down – Now."

"No." I feel a rush of air than a hard smack on my bottom.

"Ouch!"

"That is for hanging up on me." I'm more than shocked and I know he'll see this as being funny, but I don't, not really, that smarted.

"If you don't put me down, I'll do more than bloody hang up on you." I rant wriggling.

"Keep still or you'll get another."

"What!" he chuckles in his throat and I'm just about to blow my top when a door opens, and I wish the ground to open for me. Two little boys about five run out followed by a deep voice calling them.

"Peter, Stephen, wait for me."

"Daddy," they both shout stopping dead in their tracks, staring first at Edward then me red faced over his shoulder. The man appears, their Daddy, just as were on level with the door, Edward nods to him, and speaks to the boys.

"Don't be alarmed boys, I'm a fireman."

"Daddy, Daddy, he's a fireman." And the man grins - the Neanderthal. I raise my eyes and he bloody nods with a bigger grin, as Edward continues to stride down the corridor still insistent on keeping me pinned over his shoulder, and he's laughing smugly.

"I suppose you thought that was funny." No answer, but his breathing is getting deeper, and it's not from carrying me, it's from sexual tension. We stop at a door, he goes into his pocket and removes the key, slots it in and the door opens.

"Mind your head. I want you conscious." I huff, thinking, is he for real.

"I don't...." I stop as I'm now on my feet facing him, his look is more than predatory... I gulp.

"Face the wall." His tone is demanding and firm.

"What!" I breathe, shocked.

I'm spun and nearly fall, but he immediately pins my arms above my head with one hand and I can't move. My feet are splayed with his foot, as he pushes hard up against me, speaking firm.

"I said... I am going to spank that arse. And, that is what I'm going to do." And he's not asking this time, he's telling me. My heart races coupled with Goosebumps breaking out all over my skin.

"And I remember you not being averse to the idea." That very silly noise leaves my throat, the one I get in anticipation at what he's about to do. His lips move to my neck, and he knows I'm putty in his hands. The button, then the zip is undone with one hand, and my skirt falls to the floor. He breathes deep, pleased at what he sees. "Step out of your skirt." And I do. My legs again are splayed wider now. I'm still pinned with my arms above my head with his hand, it's more than a turn on, it's erotic. "Keep your hands there, above your head." I nod. One hand moves quickly cupping my sex making me fall backwards and move my hands. "Put them back." I move them back stretching up the cool plastered wall as he fondles my sex making me moan in delight. My thong is swiftly pulled falling to my ankles, and again, he commands,

"Step out." One foot at a time I step out of the thong only to be pushed back against the wall as he thrusts into my body. His hand pulls at my hair bring my head to the side as he devours my mouth with his hungry lips and rubbing himself against my bear exposed bottom. My hand moves from the wall down toward him to feel his erection, but it's grasped quickly and pinned back with the other against the wall. I gasp… feeling the same draft of air as his hand comes down quite hard onto my bottom… making me shout as I nearly orgasm.

"Oh, God. Again." he obeys with another slap followed by two fingers quickly invading me, making me scream as I push towards them wanting more. His chest moves rapidly against my back, his mouth devours my neck, and his fingers push inside me.

I squirm, moaning, my eyes roll in shear ecstasy as I'm pinned begging for more. Another hard smack sends me over the edge, leaving me almost screeching,

"I'm coming."

I'm spun to face him. Where face to face, his eyes are pure lust, his zip is down, followed quickly by his trousers then boxers, before he kicks out of them. I'm still coming panting as he places my arms around his neck and lifts me onto him. He's hard as he invades me, but his eyes have not left mine as thrusts after thrust he impatiently takes me as I plead,

"Don't stop, don't stop, ple…ase" As orgasm after orgasm invades and ignites my passion for him and he doesn't stop. My body has given over to his needs, to his wants. And this is pleasure on a different level. It's hungry, it's wanting, and needy and this is from us both. I cling to him like a limpet clinging to a rock, panting almost gasping for breath as he gives one last almighty thrust emptying inside me. His breathing is ragged and sweat covers his face and body. He moves slowly at first away from the wall, and carries me carefully towards the bed, my legs still wrapped around his waist as he holds my bottom and sits on the edge of the bed with me straddling him.

His hands cup my face, his eyes stare into mine making me stop and stare back. He doesn't speak but I can feel his words, his love and desire. My head is moved gently towards his, his mouth takes mine with all the passion in the world, as he holds me tight, not letting go, his lips don't leave mine, and I could stay like this for an eternity. He pulls away from my mouth leaving me again breathless and just stares into my eyes.

"What?" I enquire. He smiles, his head shakes looking puzzled.

"I can't believe you came all this way to see me."

"Well, you'd better had…because I did."

"Why?"

"You really need to ask?" He nods…. "Because I was missing you." His smile is tender and warm, his eyes close then open.

"Marry me, Abbie." My eyes are like saucers.

"Wh…what, did you say?" His face is so serious,

"I said. Will you, Marry me!" Tears well my eyes as I hold my hand to my mouth. I'm shaking not believing what he's just asked. A tear falls to my cheek, he wipes it with a finger as another, then another, falls as my head nods to speechless to answer.

"Is that a…yes?" he asks with a grin, and I answer with a sniff,

"Yes… God, yes, I'll marry you." I screech fling my arms so tight around his neck I nearly throttle him. And I can feel his smile against the side of my face as he hugs me and kisses me back.

Chapter 16

Sleepily I stretch out my arms feeling the empty space at my side, before I notice my hand and ring finger. There's no ring on my finger yet. We talked about that last night amongst many things and I mentioned cautiously but thoughtfully at first why I didn't want a ring not yet, and that I'd like to wait for obvious reasons. Edward was sensitive to the conversation and said he fully understood, although I wonder if he really does understand what Adam would do or say, but of course I'm not going to dwell on that. 'All in good time I told myself.' Edwards words float over me: 'all good things come to those who wait.'

I smile hearing the shower running and a delightful whistling noise coming from the occupant inside. He's happy, so, as I ponder on that thought wondering if all our days and nights are going to be like this. I can hardly believe he asked me to marry him, and honestly, I can't describe how I'm feeling apart from blissfully happy. As my eyes start to close again, I dozily stretch out my limbs then feel sore and tender. My eyes roll as I deliberate whether to join a gym when I return home just so that I may have a fighting chance of keeping up with Edward in the bedroom. My smile spreads across my face followed by a tingle down my spine as I remember last night and what a thrill it was, but I'm also aware that's he's way too much stamina.

I'm trying to doze back off, but I keep being disturbed by his whistling, followed by an outburst of song that is still coming from the bathroom. How my life has changed. I should get up really and join him, but of course he'll see it as a come on - he always does.

Passion was high last night on our return from the bar, it was hungry, needy and wanting. The second time we made love after he popped the question was, slow, gentle, passionate and very time consuming, hence my sleepy and aching limbs this morning, my eyes raise feeling sorry for Edward having to go off to work, he must be shattered.

My eyes open again and scour the room, there's half eaten food on plates, an ice bucket holing an empty bottle of champagne, glasses on the bedside table, my clothes and underwear stranded around the bedroom floor. My eyes raise again in wonderment, as I notice one of my stockings hanging from the table lamp. It looks as if we've had a party, a very raunchy party, which we haven't, but, yet again maybe we did. Edward was hungry as he'd not eaten since lunch time and to be honest, I was with all the calories I'd burned off. He ordered room service with champagne to celebrate him popping the question. He did seem rather proud of that fact and even told the receptionist our news as he ordered, stating, "Bottle of your finest bubbly, we're celebrating." He turned directly looking straight at me, "I've just asked the woman of my dreams to marry me, and she said, yes!" At that moment she must have congratulated him, because his grin was enormous before he replaced the receiver, then naked and unhurried swaggered back towards the bed making me squeal as he lunged and grabbed me, kissing and squeezing the living daylight out of me until we both fell about laughing. And of course, I puffed out my chest proudly, almost like the Robin in the garden. Why, because it made me happy. Happy because he was happy and sharing our wonderful news so freely and of course his comment *'the girl of his dreams'*. But does he know he's the man of mine?

Our food arrived and he insisted we sat up in bed eating and drinking looking out onto the roof tops of London town. I felt like Mary Poppins once again sat with him sipping our Champers, marvelling at my life, which I must confess – *'is practically perfect in every way.'*

We talked none stop until I think I fell asleep in mid-sentence on his shoulder. The bathroom door opens, and he walks out with a towel wrapped around his waist, I think he's surprised to see me awake, "Oh, your awake." I smile admiring his physique, then wonder, if he's always going to have this effect on me. "Would you like a coffee?" he asks.

"No, please, let me make it, you're going to work."

"That's what I like about you, you're always eager to please me." My eyes raise, and he laughs. "You stay there, your naked under that duvet and if you get out, well - who knows what might happen?" he laughs at his own remark. "Just this once, I'll do the coffee." He glances at the clock which in turn makes me look. It's five-thirty-five. Gosh it's early.

"Really, you're going so soon?"

"Yes, I said I wanted to finish early. So, an early start, then lunch and sights, is there anything you'd like to see?"

"No, whatever you want I'm sure it will be fab."

"Your easy pleased?" I nod taking my coffee from him before sitting up. He catches me out of the corner of his eye as he dresses as I pull the duvet over my naked chest, shaking my head, because I know that look.

"So, what time are you finishing?"

"I'll meet you in the lobby at twelve." He answers as his lips gently meet mine.

"Are you up to something?"

"Twelve and be ready on the dot."

"Bossy."

"Twelve, I said, in the lobby. Bye." And with that he vanishes through the door. He stumps me at times. He's bossy, kind, thoughtful and bloody gorgeous. I place my cup on the side and yawn, I think I'll have another hour.

I snuggle down closing my eyes falling back asleep. And no more do I remember until a knock wakes me at the door followed by someone entering.

"Hello, Room service." I pop my head out over the duvet startled by the cleaning lady glaring at me and then around the room. Her arms are full and there snuggling fresh towels, but her face says it all, and her remark stumps me, "You're not Mr Scott." I flush a little knowing what this must look like. I nod, then I think she remembers her manners. "Sorry, I shouldn't have said that, Madam." She replies with a firm but courteous tone. I somehow find myself explaining my actions, whether it's out of embarrassment I don't know, but I tell her I've a room, 1025, that she should check on her list, that I'm Edwards girlfriend, well fiancée and that I'd come down to surprise him. I think in all honesty I say it because I don't what her to think I'm a prostitute or escort. She smiles and I weakly smile back telling her it's okay to leave the room and she agrees to go and come back later. Although I'm not at all convinced that she believed my story; she must see loads of things like this. I wriggle back under the duvet until she leaves. The door closes behind her, so, I quickly sneak out of bed gather my things and dress swiftly back into the same clothes as last night, minus my underwear and stockings which are in my pocket and the basque I've squeezed into my bag. I giggle catching sight of myself in the mirror. I've got that look, you know the one, hair all over the place, shoes in hand and I look a bloody mess. I gingerly open the door to check the coast is clear, it is, so, I bomb it down the corridor looking for the stairs. Two flights down, I enter level ten and the coast is clear, so I peg it to the door, open it and fly inside standing out-of- breath but laughing, knowing I'm behaving as though I have done something really daft and naughty. I strip off my clothes and enter the bathroom, start the shower running before getting in and enjoying the warm water flowing over my tired and exhausted body. I relax, rub shampoo into my hair then spend half an hour or so, massaging shower gel into my aching muscles before leaving the bathroom in an oversize dressing gown yawning and feeling worn out. I glance at the clock it's only seven thirty. I fall backwards onto the bed wondering if anybody apart from me sleeps in this hotel, and with that thought I'm soon fast asleep. I wake refreshed. It's ten-thirty. My tummy rumbles. I need some breakfast, but I suppose the dining rooms closed now. So, I dress before ordering room service, then sit in the chair by the window waiting and watching the busy streets of London below. A knock at the door, I move to get up, but the door opens followed by a man entering. He nods, then smiles and clearly announces, "Room service, Miss."

"Thank you." I answer as he points.

"By the window as you where?" He replies pushing a small silver trolley in front of him. I nod sitting back down as he wheels it towards me. It's laid with a plate concealed with a silver dome cover. A cafeteria of steaming coffee that smells delicious, a small jug of cream or milk, and a little dish of sugar cubes with silver tongues laid at the side. It's set out to perfection. He reaches down to a shelf underneath, "Paper miss" he asks, removing it from the shelf.

"Thank you." I reply as he hands it to me very neatly folded. It appears as though it's been ironed, but then I think, that's a ridiculous notion. I rise again from my seat and reach for my bag to tip him, then realise I've the basque is inside. My face suddenly flushes, and he looks puzzled,

"I'm sorry," I say, "Umm... I've not any change now." I smile quickly trying to hide my awkwardness. "May I leave it for you later at the reception?" I glance at his name badge, "Rodney." He merely nods then turns and starts to leave the room addressing me as he goes.

"Thank you, Miss, it's alright." The door is closed quietly as I return to my breakfast. I'm glad I remember that the basque was inside, God that would have been embarrassing to say the least. But I do make a conscious note in my mind to leave it at the desk later for him when I meet Edward.

Dressed in jeans, converse, jumper and coat. I'm waiting in the lobby at 11.55am. I've left the tip for Rodney with the lady at reception as promised. I stand waiting near to the door it opens and closes as people make their way in and out of the hotel. The breeze enters with them and it's a chilly breeze today, but thankfully the rains not arrived yet. Suddenly a man strides through the door very swiftly and over enthusiastic as though he's just been blown in by the wind. He nods in my direction as he approaches then takes me by total surprise grabs me firmly by the arms and plants a cold wet kiss on my lips.

"Excuse me." I utter, "I'm waiting for someone and I don't think he'll be very pleased at you doing that." I say, shocked almost pushing him away.

"Don't care." He remarks arrogantly.

"Huh… well you should."

"Why, is he the jealous type?"

"Yes, I think he is."

"Tough." He comments back. A few people are looking at us both standing there having this *Tate r Tate* in the lobby of the Hilton. The girl on reception has raised her eyes. I laugh now not able to continue.

"Your daft." He laughs also, but of course Edward being Edward comments in his arrogant over the top tone.

"Glad to see you ready and waiting as I asked."

I knock his shoulder and he wink's.

"Where are we off too?" He takes my hand and leads me from the hotel into the Hussle and bustle of London town. The wind howls, his arm goes to my waist hugging me. I look up at him and smile.

"Hungry" I shrug my shoulders knowing I've not long tucked away a delicious potion off poached eggs and toast, although I must admit they weren't as good as his.

"I could manage a coffee while you eat." He winks leading me into a little bistro. The smell of coffee is delightful. Edward orders food and a coffee for us both as I sit watching him eat drinking my coffee.

"So, is the itinerary planned?" He nods before answering,

"The Tower - The Shard and a river cruise."

"Sounds great." He winks and continues to eat, and I just watch him, in awe, in love, feeling blessed, and never ever wanting these feelings to leave.

"Ready." he asks finishing his drink.

"Yep." I answer getting up from my seat.

We enter onto the crowded street, being pushed and shoved by locals, tourist and anyone else who happens to be on the packed pavements. Edward keeps a firm grip on my hand. Then suddenly boom, the heavens open.

"Come on!" he shouts starting to run keeping hold of my hand, and for some strange reason I begin to laugh, he looks amused as where getting drenched. He whips me quickly into a doorway and practically throws me against the door standing in front of me and protecting me from the rain. His fingers move to my cheeks as he wipes the rain and my hair from my face then slowly his lips meet mine. Where both wet and slightly out of breath stood stranded in a doorway sheltering from the down pour and thunder. I smile with a melting heart remembering the time outside the deli when I was seeing Gran off home. The couple running in the rain and then sheltering in a doorway, him protecting her and what I thought at the time as I watched them in silence.

'Was this to be my life, was this how it was meant to be. Was this to be my fate, to watch other people being happy, being in love, without ever experiencing or having love for myself?'

"You okay?" he asks puzzled gazing at my face. I nod knowing I'm more than okay. I'm Mended.

Chapter 17

We enter the lobby of the hotel after a busy memorable sightseeing tour and start heading towards the lifts chatting as we wait for it to arrive. "I'll go to my room if you don't mind and shower, then change." He says. I nod, before yawning. "Are you tired?"

"I am. Are you not?"

"A little, but a shower will wake me up, do you want to join me?" The lift arrives, and we enter continuing our conversation as we're alone.

"I'd love to." And he's that glint in his eye as the doors start to close. "But I don't think I should, because if I do, I don't think we'll eat tonight." His lip comes out in a sulk, as I press level ten.

"Damn it, Abbie, you know me so well."

"I do, Edward." I answer remembering his stamina. "I'll shower on my own thank you, in my room, and then you can call for me later - if you wish." His head bows in acceptance. "Where are we eating anyway?"

"I thought here at the hotel if that's okay?"

"That's fine it's nice and warm in here, and it'll save us from getting drenched again. Will your friends be joining us tonight?"

"I don't know, I'd not thought of that, would you mind if they did?"

"No, not at all."

"I'll ring Mike from my room and ask what they've planned."

The lift stops at my floor, the doors open, and he starts to follow me out. "I'll see you to your door." My head shakes,

"Thank you, you're such a gentleman," he grins "or is there an ulterior motive for you wanting to see me to my door?"

"No…" he says slowly and of course I know there is.

"I'll tell you what." I answer politely.

"What." He shouts as the doors start to close with him still inside.

"I'll see you later." And with that I hear a tut as the lift leaves my floor with the Horney, insatiable, Edward Scott inside. I giggle as I reach my door loving the banter, the laughter, the giggles, and the flirting that pass between us so easily.

I'm still smiling as I enter my room, then my smile gets bigger as I move towards the dressing table seeing a large bouquet of flowers. I look for a card, finding one which just says, 'congratulations. I sniff them taking in the scent. They smell so nice, and I'm a little shocked to say the least as I think there from the hotel because the message is on one of their cards. I'm still smiling as I'm getting undressed placing my clothes on a hanger and then on the outside of the wardrobe door to dry as they're still a little wet. I've just my bra and knickers on whilst I'm taking out my dress for tonight, it's nothing fancy just a little black dress I thought when packing I could either dress it up or down dependent on where he took me. Clean knickers, bra and stockings I place on the bed, before going into the bathroom to run the shower. I leave the shower and wrap one of the large white fluffy towels around myself then sit at the dressing table and start drying my hair, before placing it up twisting it into a clip and I must say it does look rather nice, and it's behaved itself for once. Next, I apply make-up before removing the towel and massaging the Chanel body lotion all over my body breathing in and knowing how nice I smell. I stand naked and start to dress fumbling with the zip. My locket I place around my neck kissing it first then place it under the dress. This is my little ritual I do if I take it off, and I never have it on show, because it's mine and personal and I don't like people asking me about it. Edward understands and always smiles or winks at me when he sees me doing it. Plus, I like it next to my heart. I sit back on the chair checking my efforts as I spray the no. 5 perfume. I nod, thinking I look okay. I smell the flowers again and smile, whispering, "I love you Edward Scott," then sit patiently waiting for him to arrive.

A knock at the door. I answer, to see him stood there in black trousers, his pale blue shirt stretched over his flexed muscles, two buttons undone just enough for me to see his olive skin. His eyes are bright and mesmerising as always, his hair messy and slightly damp from the shower, a slight stubble on his chin, God he looks edible. I fan my face with my hand making the gesture that I think he looks hot; he smirks then winks before releasing that cocky tone of his,

"I know Abbie, irresistible." I hold out my hand gesturing for him to enter. I follow behind with my tongue practically hanging out, he smells so good as he walks past, and I hope that's he's on the menu tonight. "Have you an admirer, Abbie?" he asks walking towards the dresser pointing at the flowers.

"No…I don't think so. I think they're from the hotel. Look at the card." I answer him sitting on the bed to put my shoes on while he reads the message.

"That's service."

"Umm…that's what I thought, we'll have to thank them when we go down."

"Yes. You ready?" I nod. "You look beautiful,"

"Thank you, you don't look so bad yourself." I answer kissing him on the cheek. His arms come around my waist, hugging me tight,

"God, you smell gorgeous. Are you sure you want to eat?" he murmurs grabbing at my bottom. "Look in the mirror Abbie, your arse is fantastic." He says continuing to massage it.

"Enough Mr Sex-crave spaghetti arms Scott, we can eat first then we'll see what happens." He breathes in deep and almost sticks his tongue out. I laugh, "And I'll have you know it was me who came down to London to seduce you, but I've not done that have I." He scratches his chin, shaking his head.

"So, what do you have in mind?"

"Wait and see." And for that comment I receive a slap to my bottom quite hard.

"Naughty girl. Come on let's eat and then get this party started." He wink's again with that look in his eyes that makes my knees go weak. My eyes raise as he grabs my hand, strides to the door and out on to the corridor with me in tow towards the lifts. We leave the lift and walk past the reception,

"Edward I'll just say thank you for the flowers."

"Edward." Someone calls.

"Mike be right with you." He answers. "Abbie, we can thank them later."

"Okay." I answer being guided towards Mike who's disappeared into the dining room. I enter in behind Edward to an almighty shout,

"Surprise!" my eyes are popping, totally mesmerised to see Alison, Tom, Gran, Glenda and William, Edwards parents, Veronica and Kenneth, Amelia, John, Simon and Fiona. All stood around a large table. My eyes dart to Edwards and all I can stammer is,

"Y…y…you…" He nods, "I mean, you did this? When, how…how…" he nods. I squeal as a pop from a champagne cork goes off followed by Simon spraying everyone with the contents before hollering,

"Congratulations." My heart has literally just burst as I stare at everyone smiling and laughing sprayed in the champers, then stare back towards Edward. He mimes,

"I love you." And that's it. I can't stop, call me an old romantic, but the tears flow as I hug him, but I don't whisper or mime my reply,

"I love you too." My eyes close absorbing this gesture, this love, this - I don't know, everything I suppose. I reopen them to find him on one knee holding out a small box, but I quickly close them again unable to look, because we'd talked about this. We'd agreed together, what would, or wouldn't happen if I wore a ring, and he said, *'yes'* all heartily that we'd wait, but I can't refuse him not in front of everybody. I make myself open my eyes again to find him smirking, but I don't understand why? He mimes,

"It's okay." But I feel as though it's not okay, and he knows it's not okay, or why would he say, '*it's okay*' he must sense my frustration, my confusion. I'm stuck between the devil and the deep blue sea. Every eye in the restaurant is on the pair of us, and he's still grinning holding this little black box in his hands towards me. The room's silent and it's as though everyone is holding their breath including me as I'm watching in slow motion it being opened. I don't want to look but I must, my eyes follow down to his hands, the box opens, my eyes fly to his then my head goes back and with the loudest laugh I have ever laughed releases from my lips, he stands and places the jelly ring on my finger, laughing and smiling.

"You're crazy Edward Scott." His lips go to my ear.

"That is for now, until I can put a proper ring on your finger like we agreed." My arms just fly around his body so tight that I think I wind him. The silence breaks from the room with cheering, clapping, and me I'm blissfully laughing at this silly, daft, crazy, adorable, man. Where both now being bombarded by everyone is hugging and kissing us and congratulating us. Gran squeezed me so tight I thought for a second that she'd been taking steroids. Alison deafened me screeching into my ear while hugging me. Everyone is talking laughing and hugging each other it's crazy but fantastic. We all in turn walk towards the table that's dressed with balloons, confetti, champagne on ice, and the most important people in our lives sat around. But then I realise Emily and his Gran and Lawrence aren't here.

"Edward, where's your Gran, Grandad and Emily and the children?"

"There Babysitting the nippers."

"Oh…that's kind."

"I wasn't missing out on this girl." Albert shouts over the noisy table. "Never thought this one would ever settle down." He addresses Edward. Edward just winks at Albert and everyone laughs.

"Was Emily okay staying behind?" he moves towards my ear,

"Of course, she was, because look who else isn't here."

"Jimmy." I say with a smirk.

"Precisely."

"He was also a little keen and quick to comment, saying, 'he'd help her with the children and Grandparents over the weekend.' And of course, he mentioned who'd look after Shadow. Tongue-in-cheek mind, because he knew Yvonne would have looked after Shadow if I'd have asked her to. And Emily was quick-of-the- mark to volunteer yesterday." I nod in agreement knowing it will be them two next.

"So, when did you arrange all this?"

"Friday night after I popped the question when you fell asleep on my shoulder. I needed you out of the hotel by twelve mid-day as everyone was arriving at one-ish and I couldn't risk you seeing them."

"But they got down here so fast. How?"

"I flew them all down."

"Really."

"Yes."

"Bloody hell is there no limits to your talents, Edward Scott."

"Nope, it just comes naturally." I knock his shoulder with mine laughing then look up to see Gran watching us with the most beautiful smile on her face, and to me, that is priceless.

We eventually leave the dining room after the most wonderful meal and drinks, and it now quite late. Gran, William, Glenda, and Albert went up to their room's hours ago. We're all a little drunk as we enter the lift talking noisily. Simon jibs Edward who seems to be more drunk then everyone else. Although I did see Simon John and Tom buying him shots of some kind at the bar several times. He was funny and happy, relaxed and seemed to be laughing all night.

Alison kept smiling looking at the ring because she knew the situation, and in fairness I think they all knew, maybe not as much as her, but nobody mentioned the ring, and they did all laughed at my face when Edward went down on one knee and opened the box. This however did make the evening very comfortable because nobody asked any questions. Gran, Glenda, William his parents and Albert never stopped talking and planning our wedding and I just grinned like a Cheshire cat all night long.

Us girls talked about dresses, honeymoons and all the usual stuff that accompanies a wedding. Everyone seemed to have everything planned for us and I wondered if they'd been talking about it on their flight down. But did I care. No, not in the slightest, because if this is my life now, my family, my friends then I feel truly blessed.

I watch everyone in the lift pressing different buttons to different floors. Edwards in my room tonight as he's given his room to Albert because the Hotel is full. Simon keeps jibbing him, saying,

"That's it your freedoms gone now mate." Edward nods, followed by Simon getting a slap from Fiona, but he continues, "See. Did you see that everyone? That's exactly what I mean, bro." then laughs in a very over the top drunk way. Goodbyes are said as each in turn leave the lift onto different floors and we're the last in the lift. Edwards still grinning with a drunken expression. I smile back.

"Have you had a good night." He asks, as the doors open.

"The best night ever." I answer as I walk and Edward staggers to the room. We enter, and he makes a beeline for the bed then falls backwards.

"Come on girl, over here." He says patting his chest. I throw my bag on the floor, kick off my shoes and jump on him, he laughs really loudly as his arms envelope me, followed by a most delicious kiss. "Up and strip." My head shakes. "No...Baxter, to me?" I nod. I raise from the bed he sits up staring at my face.

"My turn..." He nods.

"All yours!" he chuckles before I push him back on the bed, pulling up my dress to straddle him. His hands come up fondling my breast, then one hand glides towards the zip which is rapidly pulled down. "Lift your arm." He demands, and I do as I'm asked, lifting them above my head as he removes the dress from my body. He's now sat with me in bra, knickers and lace top stockings, straddling him. My breasts are quickly lifted from the bra, as he takes one into his mouth sucking then teasing the nip with his teeth. "God, I want to fuck you senseless." His hand cups my sex, I inhale sharply as a finger slides under the material and his finger inserts. And before I can resist, I'm flung onto my back, my knickers removed swiftly before his head lowers hastily, and his mouth starts the assault. His hands rage hungrily over my body, there quick and everywhere in seconds. His voice is determined and impatient. "Fuck, Abbie, let go. Come for me!" My hands grab the sheets as the familiar burn starts rising from my toes, my back arches, he pushes me down firmly, he's wild, giving instructions. "Come on Abbie, let me taste you." I can't stop, my back arches again, his mouth is fast his hands are quick on my skin.

"Oh, God...." I cry orgasming with force. He strips quickly, then me, as I'm coming down from the fast climax. "Turn over and get on all fours."

"No... it's my turn." His head shakes.

"No, I said, you turn over." His erection is huge, hard and almost pulsating. He takes it in his hand and begins to move over the shaft. My eyes lift to his, and his eyes beg me to do as he asks, while he tempts me masturbating, but this is meant to be my seduction.

I'm sat, he's stood almost between my legs. I smile as he continues running his hand slowly over his erection. His stare is stimulating. My hand slowly moves to my thighs pushing them slightly apart. His eyes close then open, as I start to glide it towards my sex. I swallow down, thinking, *yes*, I can do this for him. His eyes follow my hand with eagerness as mine watches his face, as I slowly run my fingers over my sex moaning slightly, he exhales watching. A murmur leaves my lips as I feel disobedient not doing as he's asked, but unhurried I move his hand away from his penis and envelope it in mine. I take my time leisurely running up and down the shaft masturbating him watching his face, his eyes close, an arousal of acceptance leaves his lips as I kiss them before slowly moving down his neck, laying small feather light kisses over his chest and working my way down towards his stomach before kneeling on the floor and gazing up towards his face, his eyes roll, his look is wanting, and waiting for me to begin. My head lowers, he moans grasping my hair and guiding me, as my seduction begins...

Chapter 18

We wake. Well I say we; Edward wakes me with a gentle kiss to my lips. "I'm just going to check on Grandad to make sure he's alright, and he's got everything he needs." I smile as he's already showered and dressed. I glance at the clock and it's eight-thirty.

"I'll get up now, why didn't you wake me?"

"Because you needed your sleep." He winks with a devilish grin, and I know with that grin what he's referring to.

"I was a busy girl last night." I say sitting up the bed naked... His eyes raise before he comments with that matter-of-fact tone.

"Yes, you were very busy, disobedient and naughty." I giggle, pulling the duvet over my body.

"Just hold out your hand for me." I look at him confused wondering if he's going to slap it, but I do it anyway. The ring is sticky and has coloured my finger. He laughs seeing it before placing it into his mouth, taking it slowly at first, before he sucks hard pulling my finger deep into his mouth removing the ring, he smirks then begins to chew. My eyes widen.

"Edward Scott." I shout, hitting him on the arm, "You've eaten my bloody ring." He nods as I stare at my bare wet finger.

"It's okay," he utters, "I've a bag full in my room, there only one-ninety-nine from the shop on the corner." He says walking towards the door still chewing our engagement ring.

"You...bloody cheap skate." I shout, hurling a pillow after him. He laughs before quickly vanishing through the door.

I'm left gobsmacked shaking my head and making my way to the bathroom, knowing I've to pack when I'm showered. We're leaving today. Edwards filming has come to an end, and he is needed back at the hospital on Monday. Albert has asked if he can drive back with us, he's not really a fan of flying. I have really taken a shine to him. And some of the things he says are quite funny. He makes me laugh. Last night he told me he'd made the flight because he did not want to miss our engagement. Which I thought was sweet, then he continued 'plus it saved him having to spend the weekend with Harriot,' he paused then added, 'he loved the nippers and liked Lawrence, but Harriot gave him a migraine.' I just giggled and told him, 'his secret was safe with me.'

I'm glad Edward's coming home. It's been strange at the house without him there. I can't believe how much I've missed him. Shadow too, he's be pining for him since he left for London. Work did fill my days, but the nights seemed so lonely without him there. I've missed our evening walks with Shadow, watching telly in front of the open fire, talking and laughing, and of course our bedtime routine.

I finish dressing, but start to feel a little sickly, although I put it down to the warmth of the bathroom. I pour myself a coffee as my mouth feels like an old sweaty flip-flop, and my head is beating nicely-along in time with the rain that's pelting at the windows. I sit in the chair and take a sip, but I must dash to the bathroom where I throw up in the loo. I return after cleaning my teeth to my mobile ringing, and it's my Gran, I swipe the screen to hear her voice,

"Hi, good morning, sweetheart."

"Hi, gran, are you okay?"

"Yes, are you."

"Umm…a little sickly this morning."

"Oh dear, go back to bed for a while."

"I think I will. I'm just waiting for Edward to get back, he's nipped up to see Albert."

"That's nice. Do you want me to come down?"

"No, I'll be okay. Plus, it might be a bug, and I'd not want you to catch it."

"Oh dear…" but her tone says, hangover.

"I'll be in work on Monday for a few hours to catch up."

"Me too. Have we to pick you up then? Say Nine

nine-thirty."

"Please."

"I need to go dear; Glenda and William are meeting me for breakfast and then a taxi to the airport. Are you coming down for anything?"

"No, I don't think so."

"Okay, my love, I see you on Monday then."

"Yes, Monday." She hangs up. I smile at her words she still wants to come and look after me at the age of 26. No sooner have I place my phone down it goes again.

"Morning." Alison says, bright and breezy.

"Morning." I almost whisper.

"Oh dear, Abbie...hangover?"

"No. I didn't drink that much last night."

"Huh, really who are you kidding. Have you been sick?"

"Yeah, and I hate being sick."

"No point asking you then if you're coming for bacon and eggs?"

"Sod off, that was cruel. I'm going now." She's laughing.

"Sorry couldn't resist it."

"I'm going to go back to bed I think, for an hour."

"Best thing for a hangover, sleep it off." I just roll my eyes. "Are we still meeting on Wednesday?"

"Yes of course."

"Okay, honey, I'll see you on Wednesday. The party was fantastic by the way last night."

"It was, wasn't it, I'm a very lucky lady."

"Not this morning you're not." She answers laughing.

"Bye Alison, see you Wednesday."

"Bye lovey." And with that we both hang up at the same time, and I'm sure the pair of us are smiling at each other's comments. But I suppose that's what friends do, take the micky. Edward arrives back, he's also bright and breezy, which in fairness I don't think is fair because, I didn't drink half as much as them two did last night.

"Good, you're up. Breakfast?" I shake my head wishing everyone would stop mentioning bloody breakfast.

"I don't think I can." I answer retching a little.

"No…why not?" I just roll my eyes thinking he must have a hardened Liver or something. "Did you drink too much last night, Abbie?"

"I felt alright when I got up, but I think it might be the heat of the bathroom."

"I think you've a hangover, have you been sick?" I nod pathetically, his eyes raise.

"I didn't drink that much Edward. Well, not half as much as you did." He walks over towards me going into his pocket.

"Hold out your hand." So, I do as he asks, and he places another jelly ring on my finger.

"You're daft you are, but you know that already, don't you?"

"I do, and I'm especially daft around you. Would you mind if I take my Grandad for breakfast?"

"No, not in the least, you just go."

"Do you want anything bringing up from the dining room?"

"No, thank you.

"Some iced water maybe and paracetamol?" he answers with a smirk, and I've no come back, because I think he's right, I do feel hungover. "Why don't you go back to bed."

"I've my packing to do."

"I'll do that for you, don't worry, you lay down and sleep it off."

"Are you sure?"

"Yes, of course I am."

"Thank you."

"No, worries - come" he takes my hand walking me to the bed. I get in and he covers me. "I'll open the window and let in some fresh air, before I nip to the shop to get you some drugs." My eyes close and I'm soon back asleep. I'm only asleep a short while when I'm woken by a soft voice.

"Here Abbie take these." He's sat on the side of the bed next to me holding a glass of water and two pills. "Take them and go back to sleep." I nod, sit and take the pills, sip the water as he holds the glass. He kisses my forehead gently and pulls the duvet back over me. "Close your eyes sweetheart" and I do what I'm told, which I think shocks him. "I'm going to get grandad." I answer him in my head as I'm tired and still feel sick. I hear the door close quietly and then no more.

"Oh, good morning Miss I'm sorry, I did knock, but nobody answered." I open one eye startled to see a young girl stood at the foot of the bed. "Do you wish me to come back? Aww the flowers look nice. Do you like them? I put them in your room yesterday." I nod, wondering if she is going to come up for air. But, no she doesn't. "Well would you like me to start in the bathroom?"

"No, it's fine…" I try to focus on her name badge.

"Jenny." She answers seeing me looking.

"Where, leaving today."

"Oh, dear are you not happy, are you ill." I roll my eyes thinking, she's asking to many questions. But then she smiles, and it seems genuine.

"No, I'm fine thank you." And I must admit I do feel a little better, but my heads still banging.

"Did you drink too much?" She asks nodding her head answering her own question. "I heard about the engagement, aww...bless yah, how nice." Although I wish everyone would stop saying I drank too much, because honestly. I didn't, but her second comment does somewhat make me smile as she's about seventeen but sounds seventy, and she's very forward.

"Thank you. Jenny would you thank the hotel manager for the flowers." I ask. She laughs loudly which rings through my head like a bag full of marbles.

"The hotel. Hell, they're not from the hotel."

"Oh, I just presumed they were, because of the card." I answer her getting out of bed.

"May I look?" she asks walking towards them.

"Please."

"Yes, it's one of our cards but the Hotel never send flowers, well not unless you're a VIP. Are you a VIP?"

"No, Jenny I'm not." I answer then think I wonder if the hotel thinks Edward is a VIP because of the filming.

"A secret admirer then?" I shake my head knowing nobody knows I'm down here and to my knowledge I don't have a secret admirer either. "Would you like me to see what I can find out, a little detective work perhaps." I now want to laugh as she's serious and is almost begging me to let her as she nods her head for me to say, yes.

"If you wish."

"I'm on it." And with that she scarpers fast out of my room. I sit on the side of the bed rolling my eyes but don't have time to think about that now as I need to pack. Edwards ringing my mobile. I swipe the screen,

"Hi, are you okay?"

"Good, you're up, are you feeling any better, have you packed?" he seems a little stressed rhyming of questions.

"Yes, I've packed, why is there something wrong?" He breathes out before answering

"It's grandad, he's not feeling very well."

"But, is he okay?"

"I'm not sure, I think so, he could've just overdone it last night, but I'd prefer to get him home."

"Yeah, yeah, that's fine."

"I'm going to take him down to the car then I'll come and get you."

"I'll meet you there at the car."

"You can't, I've got the pass card with the code."

"Okay, I'll walk to the lift now and wait for you."

"Yeah, good idea."

I walk out the room and head for the lifts but meet Jenny walking down the corridor pushing her cleaning trolley. She smiles and makes a beeline for me.

"Miss, I found out for you who the flowers where off," her eyes glance towards them, which I'm holding by the handle in their box.. I continue walking,

"I'm sorry Jenny, I'm in a bit off a rush."

"It's fine Miss, I'll walk with you and tell you. They're from your brother." I look at her stunned, placing the flowers down as I wait outside the doors for the lift to come.

"I don't have a brother."

"Well that's what Daniel just said to me. He said they were delivered by a courier who asked for one of our cards, gave the message and said if she asks tell her they're from her brother, and that was that." I shrug my shoulders thinking that is a strange message. Then wonder if she got mixed up, and the courier meant Edwards brother. The doors open, Edward's inside with Albert, and I must confess he does look tired and pale.

"Abbie." He says acknowledging me stood there before walking a little out of the lift to take my case. I pick up the flowers, walking in but not before turning and thanking Jenny. She smiles, saying "Your welcome miss, safe journey home."

"What was all that about?"

"The flowers Edward" I gesture towards them. His chin lifts. "I asked her to thank the hotel for us. but she said they were from my brother which I think…." I stop talking as Albert starts coughing.

"Okay, grandad? "

"Yeah. I'm fine lad, just a little parched."

"I'll stop when we get out of the centre and get you a drink."

"Hey, lad you fuss too much." I smile at Albert who winks at me. Edward looks worried. I squeeze his hand to let him know I'm there. Because were the same. I worry about my gran just like that.

We leave the lift and enter the underground car park. Edward slots a card into a machine then presses four numbers into the pad before the gate releases. We walk through towards the car. I'm helping Albert into the front seat while Edward puts my case and flowers in the boot. His and Alberts stuff are already in.

"Aww, thank you lass. He does fuss far too much, although I should tell him I'm coughing because I had a cigar last night. But if I tell him that he'll go off on one."

"You don't need to tell me grandad, I heard."

"Now, Edward, not in front of Abbie." Albert grins at me - I grimace back, and Edward gives us both a withering look, but I think he does seem a little more relaxed knowing it's probably the cigar and not his heart as I climb into the back of the BM.

"Ready." He addresses us both in an authoritative tone.

"Yes." I answer.

"Aye-aye captain." Albert replies, with a chuckle. Edwards eyes raise which makes me snigger, and he stares at me through the mirror, so, I just raise my eyes.

"We'll speak about this when we get home, grandad." He drives out onto the busy street. I gaze out of the window and Albert stays quiet and to be honest I feel as though I've just been told off. The rain is lashing down on the windscreen. People running here, there and everywhere dashing in and out of shops to shelter from the weather. He's concentrating on the roads and busy traffic, and off course the rain is making it twice as difficult to see. We leave London centre heading towards the motorway. Albert sighs,

"Okay." Edward asks him.

"I'm fine honestly, I've no pain, no breathlessness, I'm just tired."

"Have a nod then."

"Umm…" he answers, and it sounds as if he's sulking, because he's been told off too. I smile at Edward who catches my eye in his mirror. I know he's grumpy because he cares and to be honest Albert shouldn't have had the cigar he was told not to. But what do you say to a seventy-year-old man who wants a cigar? No, you can't?

"You have a sleep too Abbie, it will do you the world of good." He winks because, I know he really thinks I've a hangover. "How is your head." I sigh now. "Better, thank you."

"Good. Music?"

"Please." The radio comes on, and I sit listening to the songs looking out of the window. Were quiet because Alberts dosed off. I yawn feeling sleepy.

"Get your head down, I'm fine listening to the radio."

"Okay, if you're sure." I make myself comfy and pull Edwards coat over my shoulders that's on the back seat. I can smell his aftershave on it as my eyes start to close and I'm soon fast asleep.

The car pulls up at the little church. It's snowing, and everything is white and glistening. William smiles. "Are you ready lass." I nod with a huge grin. Alison is waiting in her black gown and white fur shrug. She looks cold.

"I'm ready William." She opens the car door and helps me out adjusting my dress. Williams teeth chatter, then he shivers.

"It's brass monkeys out here." I nod but surprisingly I'm warm. I can hear music coming from inside the church as we walk up the small path. It's upbeat pop music, I stare at Alison who shrugs her shoulders, as I think it's strange music to be playing at a wedding. As we approach the large oval oak door's they open but there's nobody there. The vestibule is arranged with flowers, Christmas flowers for the season. A large wreath hangs on the entrance door to the church. The smell of pine- cones flood our senses. I can hear voices over the pop music coming from inside. The door opens to the main church, I see Edward and Simon stood at the altar. They turn to look. The wedding march starts. William winks and takes my arm. Alison lets out a little squeal from behind us. I take a deep breath as we enter and slowly start walking up the centre aisle. All eyes are on us, but mine are on Edwards, he looks stunning, but nervous for one who is usually so confident. His smile is huge, as I walk towards him. Gran and Glenda are sat on the front row. Gran smiles with tears in her eyes. Glenda wipes a tear away with a tissue. My heart could not grow any larger. I squeeze grans hand as she holds it out to me as I pass. He stares at me, smiles, then whispers, "You look beautiful." A tear hits my eye. I feel so emotional to be marrying this beautiful, amazing man. The priest asks,

"Who gives this woman to this man?"

"I do." William answers, his voice appears croaky, before he releases my arm taking my hand and placing it in Edwards, then turns and sits with Gran and Glenda. Alison stands at my side holding my delicate bouquet of flowers.

The priest begins his wedding sermon as we stand facing each other. He stops for a brief second, and his eyes move to Edwards then to my vail. Edward acknowledges him with a nod, and slowly moves forward taking the vail into his hands, as he slowly starts to lift it, I close my eyes holding my breath. I feel it move over my face; I open my eyes to look at him. I freeze, it's not Edward, it's Adam, what is happening...God, no, it can't be him not again. My eyes now scour the empty church, the priest has gone, it's cold, and the once beautiful flowers have started to wither. I gasp for breath then my eyes open.

"Hell are you alright Abbie, you made me jump." I just stare at him in the mirror. Because I've just realised who the flowers are off. God, why did we not think, after all that he's done to us, why...why did we not realise. *From your brother,* Jenny said, and I thought Edwards brother, Simon, but why on earth would he send flowers when he was already down here. Edward doesn't know what Jenny really said, for one I don't think he was listening to me and two we were both wrapped up with Albert at the time. And why is he in my head again – why, when I'm so happy. Am I ever going to be free of him? "Abbie!" he asks as I've still not answered. But I can't answer him, and I can't tell him either. My head is whizzing, wondering and worrying what Adam is up to. Why on earth can't he just leave me alone.

Chapter 19

Edward has dropped the cases in the hallway, with the flowers next to the ottoman. I glare at them knowing exactly what I'm going to do with them. He's taken Albert back to his mother's house so he's going to be some time returning. I pick up the flowers and walk down the hall towards the kitchen, the house seems silent without Shadow, as he's still with Jimmy.

I walk into the kitchen placing the flowers on the side, but then think, No. Do it now - no time like the present and I don't want a reminder of them or him. I take them into the utility room, open the bin and throw them inside glaring at them in disgust and the contempt in which they were sent, slamming the lid shut, and knowing how easily Adam puts me in a bad mood. Edward still thinks I've a hangover, because of how quiet I was in the car, after I'd realised Adam had sent the flowers and of course that dream. That was bizarre to say the least. Lovely to begin with but the end well…it's as though my sub-conscious was warning me, telling me, too wake up and smell the coffee. I blow out an exacerbated breath whilst walking back into the kitchen. I check the kettle for water and flick the switch. I'll ring him soon, find out what time he's back and what he wants to do for dinner.

My appetites returned and I'm a little hungry. I open

the fridge but it's like Old Mother Hubbard's. Maybe I should have stocked up before going away, but then again, I wasn't meant to be back until Monday night. I check the freezer, meat, some meals made by Yvonne, but nothing I fancy, so I take two slices of bread from the packet and place them to toast, finish making my coffee as we've milk and sit eating the toast and drinking my brew. When I've finished, I place the plate and cup into the sink and return to the bedroom to empty my case and Edwards bags.

I've not much washing but Edward seems to have a bit. His shirts and trousers I place in the basket for the dry cleaning as Yvonne takes those. I've also put in my Prada suit and silk blouse and the little black dress hoping he doesn't mind but I'll make sure to ask him on his return. The rest I take to the utility area and set the machine going. I return to the kitchen pick up my mobile and dial his number. I fancy a walk to the pub, as my so-called hangover has now left, plus it will blow the cobwebs and thoughts away. He doesn't answer so I leave a message.

3.35pm. "Hi, just wondering what you'd like to do for dinner. I fancy a walk to the pub now it's stopped raining. Call me back please when you get this. Bye, love you."

The washings on and I potter around tiding the kitchen then walk into the lounge. It's all clean and tidy as I did it before I went away. I sit on the sofa and switch the telly on. It's the news channel, he's talking to the weatherman about the devastation the rain has caused over the weekend with floods in parts. They now switch to a meteorologist to explain.

"Britain's weather is down to the fact that it's an island and where it is positioned, between the Atlantic Ocean and a large land mass, continental Europe. Britain is under an area where five main air masses meet. An air mass is a large body of air…" I think at this point she's lost me, and probably most of the population in England, because all we really want to know about the weather is… is it going to rain today. I laugh returning to the kitchen to make another coffee, knowing if Edward was watching he'd be scrutinising everything she was saying, and more than likely disagreeing as well. The washer has finished, and I go through the clothes putting some to air, and the others in the dryer. I glance at the bin hoping he's not going to look inside, but there again why should he look in the bin. Although I need a good excuse as to where the flowers are if he asks about them. My phone bleeps, a message, I check and it's Edward.

4.30pm: Hi, yes should be back for 6ish, pub sounds good. Grandad settled and fine, checked him over and all obs are stable. Setting of soon. Love yah too x

I smile at the text, as I return upstairs to potter then get ready. I take out a skirt, blouse and jacket for myself nothing to formal for tomorrow as I don't think I've anything scheduled. Edward I'm not sure about because they asked him to go in. I've taken his blue pinstriped suit from the rail, a white shirt along with his blue tie, hanging them alongside mine. Trousers and a jumper for tonight for me, and Edward can choose himself if he wants to change. I remove my locket and place it next to the gummy ring, before making my way into the bathroom to shower. On with the shower cap as I only washed my hair this morning and I've not really got time again.

Finished, locket in place and gummy ring back where it belongs and sat waiting with a coffee in the kitchen for him to return home. I've booked a table at the pub because it's Sunday and they get packed, but I'm not surprised the food is to die for. Sunday roast with all the trimmings, fresh and homemade, and the puddings - well that is a different story. The sticky-toffee sponge and custard has won awards. The chef is portly to say the least, and Edward said, 'it was a good sign and that you should never trust a skinny chef.' I laughed, and commented, 'it wasn't very PC,' he agreed with me and laughed, saying, 'no it wasn't, but that's what his Grandad Albert always use to say. And for some strange reason the silliest things seem to stick in your mind.

I agreed remembering silly things my grandparents had said to me. And I still say some of them now. The door opens, and I hear him.

"Honey I'm home," I smile as he strides into the kitchen. "Where are the cases and flowers." God, he doesn't miss a bloody trick he's far too smart sometimes for his own good.

"I've moved them, done the washing and the dryers on." His eyes raise as he walks towards me, kisses me on the cheek before taking my coffee and taking a long slurp then comments.

"I knew It was the right decision, marrying you." I quickly change the subject fast before he mentions the flowers again. He throws post on the counter, "some for you,"

"I'll look at them later. Are you going like that? I've booked a table for seven."

"Yeah, come on then if were walking." I'll grab a coat and my boots. "How's Albert."

"He's fine. The cigar, rich food and flight made him tired."

"Did the flight leave on time?"

"Yes, Mum said it was a bit ropey as there was a lot of turbulence. Have you not spoken with your gran?"

"No, is she okay?"

"Yes, sorry she's fine, I just thought you might have rung her."

"Should I have done? I mean I have spoken with her this morning, and I'm meeting her tomorrow, she's picking me up."

"I thought you were off tomorrow."

"No, I'm going in with being away, I feel a little guilty plus I'm only doing a few hours."

"Okay, lets walk and talk." he says as I'm just fastening my coat. We enter out into the cool, dark evening making our way down the drive and out through the gates holding hands. "Umm…Abbie, I think another option for a ring is needed this is quite sticky."

"I know, but I don't like being without it now." He laughs

"You don't need a ring to know I love you, or do you?"

"No, don't be silly."

"Good." He says taking my finger again and placing it in his mouth,

"No." I screech but it's too late it's gone again, then he starts running in front laughing his head off. I chase him, he stops, and grabs hold of me kisses me firmly on the mouth. I can taste the strawberry on his lips. He's still laughing as we continue to walk towards the pub. We talk all the way there about our weekend and he's trying to scare me with stories from the Tower of London as we walk down the lane that leads to the pub. It's very dimly lit and isolated with fields of nothing at either side. A few old lamps sparsely light the way. A huge lantern hangs from the side of the leaning stone porch, and the sign swings above it that reads: The pub. That's what it's called, but back in the day as Edward informed me on our first visit it was a coach house for change overs. And pirates used to hide out with their bounty in the stables. But that was not confirmed. I think he was making that last bit up. It's very quaint both inside and outside. He continues with his tales and scaring me as we walk towards the light.

"I'm not listening to you, Edward Scott."

"Are you not?"

"No, and you're not scaring me in the slightest I've heard your tales before."

"Really, so why are you gripping on to my hand so tightly." I stare at him and he's that smug grin on his face.

"Shut up." He laughs loudly and squeezes my hand.

"I knew you were scared really." I poke my tongue out, he laughs even harder. "Come on" he shouts, "someone's behind us," and I know he's joking but somehow when someone says something like that, there's always that little self-doubt in the back of your mind, his grip is tight, and he starts to run, and I don't really have much of a choice now as to run or fall flat on my face. So, I run with him giggling, with my heart beating ten-times-to-the-dozen. We enter the leaning porch panting, out of breath, as a couple are leaving through the door holding it open for us.

"Thank you" I say, and Edward nods his reply.

"Your welcome." They reply.

We walk to the bar saying we've booked and are escorted through. It so nice and cosy and very busy, but we get the last seated table next to the fire.

"Edward, hi." A lady says as we walk past.

"Hi." He answers and stops, before introducing me.

"Abbie, this is Laura," She smiles, "and Jerry, her husband they have the farm next to us, were we get our eggs and meat from."

"Your eggs are the best I've ever tasted."

"Thank you." Laura replies.

"You'll have to come around for drinks soon Edward and bring, Abbie." Jerry asks.

"Thanks, we will." They nod at each other as we continue to our table. A lot of people seem to know Edward in here. They greet him and smile at me. I've been a couple of times with him, but it was never this packed before, busy, yes, but it's bursting at the seams tonight.

"Can I take your order, please." A chap asks quickly, before our bums have even touched the seat.

"What's the rush Dave, can't we get a drink first?"

"You can Edward, but where stopping the food at seven-thirty tonight and finished eating for eight."

"Why?"

"Final of the quiz tonight and you know what that's like, God, some of them take it so seriously."

"We best order then."

"Menu, Abbie?" Edward asks.

"No, I know what I'm having. Have you any sticky-toffee pudding left?" Dave nods. "Then I'll have a small roast beef dinner, please,"

"All the trimmings?" he asks.

"Please, and the sticky toffee pudding with custard for afters." Edwards eyes raise.

"Same for me then."

"A small one, Edward?"

"Don't be daft Dave, normal for me, and extra custard."

"What on your Yorkshire," he says laughing walking towards the kitchens.

"Drink, Abbie." He asks standing to go to the bar.

"Just a soft drink for me please."

The food arrives, and it is delicious as always, small gosh it's massive. Roast beef, homemade Yorkshire puddings, roasted parsnips and potatoes, cauliflower cheese, sprouts, broccoli mangetout and all cooked to perfection, and the gravy well I'm sure it's a secret recipe because I've never tasted gravy quite like it before. I can't manage it all and leave quite a bit, Edward comments.

"Are you not hungry?"

"I'm saving room for the pud." He smiles. The pudding arrives, and it melts in my mouth and tastes divine. I murmur all the way through as Edward watches me tucking away the full bowl. I slump back, miming to him. I need to undo my trousers. His eyes glance as if to say, what here in the pub. I laugh quietly because he's turned my innocent remark into a sexual one.

"Do you want to stay for a bit and listen to the quiz?"

"It's up to you, I don't mind in the slightest."

"Another drink then first."

"May I have a coffee, please." He nods and goes again to the bar. I sit taking in the room. Everyone's chatting away to each other. I watch Edward at the bar he chats and greets people. Points in my direction several times and it's evident he's talking about me. I do feel a lot more relaxed now, and I've not thought about the flowers, and Edward thank goodness hasn't mentioned them. I love this being out with him, although I like our cosy nights in as well, and I've loved our weekend. He arrives back with a beer and a coffee. And he must read my thoughts,

"It's nice in here don't you think?"

"Yes, its lovely."

"Taxi home or do you want to walk."

"I think walk. We need to walk that massive dinner off before we go into a food coma."

"Walk it is then, drink up and let's set off before the quiz really gets under way, you never know, they might start brawling."

"I'm sure they won't"

"Don't bank on that thought Abbie, serious stuff, finals especially in a village, with a trophy up for grabs. You should know that." I laugh thinking, yes, he's probably right. Although I've never been to the local pub in my village, just Gran and Grandad's deli and I've never joined the quiz team, it seems I haven't done a lot of things, but that is about to change. I like meeting people. I like talking to people, and I like making new friends. And I especially like doing all those things with Edward. Making new memories.

Chapter 20

Another Monday morning and the start of a brand-new week, and the start of Edward back home where he belongs. I was up first on guard of the utility room as I didn't want him going in there. He's not mentioned the flowers thank God, but I still don't want to take that chance. He'll flip if he knows there from Adam. My face scowls at the thought of him, and him sending the flowers playing his senseless mind games. Stupidly, I've been into the bin several times already making sure there still there, but I'm not sure why I keep doing it. Edward enters the kitchen just as I'm leaving the utility again. He's dressed in the pinstripe and looks immaculate to say the least. I'm still in Pyjamas and slippers with my famous bed head hair, to put that phrase politely. But he kisses me all the same.

"Good morning is this mine?" he asks picking up a freshly brewed coffee.

"Of course."

"What time are you in?"

"Grans not picking me up until nine - nine-thirty."

"Part timer." He chuckles, "Good job I'm going in on time, someone has to pay the bills." He utters walking towards the dishwasher.

"Here leave that I'll tidy round before my shower." I say quickly as he's walking past the utility. I internally roll my eyes knowing I'm being bloody stupid because he hardly ever goes in there unless he's going into the cellar for something which again isn't too often.

"Good to see your already playing the wife." My eyes raise, and he laughs. "Dinner tonight, what do you fancy doing?"

"I'll cook if you like seeing I'm only in for a few hours, and I wouldn't want you thinking, I'm not pulling my weight." I answer as straight faced as I can.

"I'd…" I laugh. And he slaps my bottom.

"You pull your weight in other ways." I'm not at all sure I'm taken to that comment, and it shows evidently on my face. "That was a joke, Abbie."

"It's a good job it was, or you'd be sex starved, as well as bloody hungry."

"Feisty as ever." I receive a kiss. "I'll see you tonight. I shouldn't be later than five-ish." I smile as he picks up his briefcase and phone. "Jimmy might drop Shadow off this afternoon, so we can go for a walk before or after dinner if you'd like that." I grin because this is perfect. I love doing this. Walking in the evening, cosy dinners, watching telly – it's a nice life. "Your posts here from the weekend."

"Thanks." I glance at the one on top which is from uni. "My papers to say I've left the course, probably."

"Right, I'm off."

"A kiss before you leave?"

"Off course, any chance for a quick grope and kiss." I cough,

"A kiss that's it…" I wink, and he smirks, "And if you're a good boy I'll see what I can do for that uncontrollable sex-drive of yours maybe later tonight."

"I like the sound of that. It's a date." So, a small kiss I get but a huge grin before he turns and walks out the door, shouting he's taking the 4 x 4 today. I giggle knowing there is a fine line between his stomach, and sex, but if it came down to it, sex would win, and he'd starve. I make my way to the coffee machine pour another to take upstairs.

Dishwashers loaded, kitchen cleaned, laundry folded, steaks out of the freezer for dinner. The salad drawers empty, but Yvonne's due today so it'll be restocked as she visits the farm on Mondays, also my haste to empty the bin to the outside one, so there's no questions, because I'm sure she'd ask if she saw the flowers, and fibbing is not one of my forte's. Then I think, who the hell am I kidding, I've been fibbing most of my life.

9 am. I sit at the counter and open my mail. I was right the letter was from uni saying, they'd taken me off the course and wished me all the best for the future. Which I thought was nice. A couple are junk mail, which I rip up and place to the side. One from the solicitors, his solicitors, his

firm. Holden Brown and Lord. I blow out a grimace of breath wondering if it's the divorce papers, because what else would they be writing to me about. My heart quickens as I turn it over to open, my fingers fumble and shake because this could be it, the start of the rest of my life. I rip at the seal placing my fingers inside but don't feel a letter but instead bits of paper. I pull some from the envelope.

"Bastard" I shout out, emptying the contents onto the top. There the divorce papers alright, ripped up, a yellow post-it-note is stuck to one with the words:
FUCK-YOU! In capitals.
My chair flies out beneath me. I'm livid and ranting,

"Bastard, bastard." Although should I really be surprised at this? What the hell is Edward going to say, do I hide this from him as well. Do I take it to Mrs Bradshaw and show her, do I ram it down Adams throat? God, just as everything was falling into place he's back like the incurable disease, the disease I thought I was cured off, that I'd got the all clear from, but what a silly little girl I've been. I walk into the utility and open the bin and see the flowers, throwing the pieces of paper in, the yellow post-it lands on the top with the words,
FUCK YOU! staring me in the face.

"No fuck you, Adam Lord" I shout pulling them back out and ramming them into my pocket. Some have fallen to the floor and I fumble picking them up as my hands are shaking with adrenaline. The intercom goes. My eyes close its Gran. I run back to the kitchen grab my bag, keys and head for the door, stopping for a brief second to calm myself down.

The pieces of paper and post-it-note in my pocket and no bloody idea what-the-heck to do. I press the gate and answer,

"Hi, drive up I'm on my way down to meet you." I walk out, slam the door shut and don't give poor William the chance to answer. It's brisk, a cold nip hits my face as I march down the drive seeing the Bentley driving towards me. It's freezing I've not even got my coat on just the skirt suit and blouse and my heels are difficult on the gravel. But I'm not thinking rational. I'm fuming, but I need to calm down. I take a few more deep breaths of the brisk air and as it enters hitting my lungs, my hands begin to steady. The Bentley pulls to myside and the window goes down,

"Abigail, where is your coat?" I pull in another breath, answering

"Good morning, what a fresh day." I reply climbing into the back, as that ever-familiar tone of lying comes from my lips once more. "I needed that brisk blast of air gran, to wake me up especially after the busy weekend." She smiles and turns back to face the front but comments,

"Yes, but you still should have worn a coat." I nod, knowing I'm doing it again, lying because of him, hiding the truth, because what-the-hell do, I do? Do I tell her. Tell Edward about the flowers, the dream, the ripped-up divorce papers, the post-it-note. Adam's cornering me again.

"What a fantastic weekend, Abbie. Do you know Glenda and your Gran have never stopped talking about it since we got back? He's a nice lad is Edward." I nod.

"He is Abbie, He's lovely." Gran adds. Again, I nod as William looks at me in the mirror, he can sense that I'm not alright because, I'm not babbling or chatty, so he nods discreetly a sign to ask if I'm okay. My eyes close briefly remembering my weekend, my family, Edwards family, our friends making me realise he can't get away with this. I can't even wear my jelly ring now that we're home. But I shouldn't have to wear a jelly ring. I should be able to wear a ring that Edward has chosen for me, for all to see. I must put an end to this. To his senseless mind games, his control, his attempts to continue running my life. And it must be today. I finally answer.

"Yes, William I'm fine. And yes, it was a fantastic weekend." I muster with the most convincing of tones trying to calm my temper so not to give myself away, not to hint that what I'm about to do because anyone who truly knows Adam will also Know I'm about to enter the Lion's Den.

Unarmed and unprepared, but with one thought, and one thought only. Revenge.

Chapter 21

The drive in with Gran and William was hard to say the least and it was mostly in silence especially from me as my brain is mashed with thoughts. Thoughts that spin faster than a gamblers roulette wheel. Have I or haven't I.

I'm so irritable with a host off emotions soaring through me and I've no concentration span. Every time I try to start an invoice, a costing, my mind soon flitters back to Adam. My hands shake every time I think of the divorce papers ripped up, the attached post-it-note, those flowers, his deception, although it's not like before, my hands aren't shaking with fear, they're shaking out of anger. The phone rings slightly distracting me.

"Good afternoon, Baxter's deli, may I help you." Tracy answers making me wonder how it's got to afternoon already, however I seem to switch off from her conversation trying to focus on the job-in-hand, but it's warm in here today and stuffy, it must be the smallest office out of all the chains, I think fanning my face with a card from the desk, before reaching for my water bottle, but grimace because it's empty. Now on a normal day these things wouldn't bother me in the slightest, but today every little thing seems to be either irritating me or making me lose track of what I'm meant to be doing. I know Tracy's picked up on it, as we're usually quite chatty with each other.

"Abigail, would you like me to get you another bottle of water and something to eat?" she asks replacing the receiver.

"Thank you," and I was about to add an apology for my mood, but Gran walks through the door. I know it's her without having to turn, her scent hits my nostrils, the tap and rhythm of her kitten heels make on the wood floor alert my senses and It's calming. I've always been able to tell it was her, even from a very young age, her smell, her noise. Maybe I do have a sixth sense, then I remind myself why I'm in this mood, so that confirms I've no sixth sense at all. More like a daft, stupid one.

"Hi, how are you getting on?" She asks continuing to walk towards me.

"It's taking me sometime today." I answer turning to face her.

"Are you still not well?"

"I'm okay."

"Really, you do seem flushed and not your usual self." She comments placing a finger on the screen at an entry I've just made. "I don't think we can charge a hundred and fifty pounds for a Scone?"

"Can't we?" I say a little weakly seeing my mistake, and it's true I am flushed and not at my best.

"No, dear one-pound-fifty, max, I think." Her eyes raise as she places a sympathetic hand on my shoulder.

"Sorry." I breathe changing the decimal point and deleting a couple of zeroes.

"Are you sure you're alright. I mean you're usually bob-on with all the figures."

"I am, It's just…" I stop as I nearly blurt out my true thoughts.

"It's just what, dear…you can tell me you know that. Don't you?" God, she knows me so well when I'm hiding something. She was one of those when I was growing up, I couldn't get away with anything. As she often reminded me - 'yes, yes, I've done that got the t-shirt' I change my tactic's quickly to avoid a digging session.

"I know Gran. I think to be honest I'm still feeling a little unwell and I'm warm."

"Well, why don't you get off home I can ask Ted to finish up in here." My head shakes my reply. "Okay, well, why don't you put your jacket on and go and have five minutes outside, get some fresh air and eat something? I'm just popping to Baron Road."

"Why, what's wrong?"

"Oh, nothing really it's just the new manager is having a little difficulty with some ordering."

"Do you want me to go instead?"

"No, I've rang William and he's picking me up shortly, I'll not be too long, about an hour or so."

"I'll grab a sandwich then and wait for you to get back. I can finish up in here and I'll probably feel better after something to eat and some fresh air, plus Ted's really busy downstairs." I say all this because, I know I don't want to go home not really, to start thinking on things although I'm not doing a good job at not thinking about Adam here either. So, I take my own advice, pushing out my chair and placing my jacket on, leaving the office and Gran collecting her files. I head down the narrow winding steps into the hustle and bustle of the deli to be greeted by staff and Ted commenting as I walk past,

"Abbie, congratulations." I raise my head to acknowledge them but continue walking without answering since I know I shouldn't feel like this. I should be buzzing, showing off my ring, shouting, 'Thanks.' I inhale another deeper breath closing my eyes briefly as I've this impossible urge burning way down in my gut, twisting and bending, knotting the very insides of me, making me feel physically sick. And the reason for this - is that I want to go to his office and ram those papers down his ugly, disgusting throat but my sub-conscious is nagging me, don't do it Abbie, but the urge is strong, much stronger than what my sub-conscious is telling me to do.

"Hi, Abigail, your gran said you were out here. Your water." She smiles, as I take it from her. "do you want me to put your sandwich in the office?"

"Thank you." I reply taking a drink. I shiver pulling my jacket around me tightly before placing my hands into the pocket and feeling the paper and the post-it-note. And that's it, it's like a red rag to a bull. "Tracy." I call before she walks back inside, "Please can you tell my gran, if she asks, that I've gone for a walk to clear my head."

"Of, course I will."

"Thank you." I answer walking through the little car park and out onto the high street. I take deep breaths with every step of my foot on the pavement. My heart races with adrenaline, as I know I'm walking into that Lion's den, which 'yes' is reckless, irresponsible and crazy, but I can't take anymore.

As I stand outside Holden - Brown and Lord reaching for the handle to enter I feel physically sick, my hand trembles as I grasp it before turning it to open, although courage comes from somewhere, that's if I can call it courage.

Memories suddenly flood back as I find myself standing in the reception area. Kimberley's at her desk, her head lifts, her eyes meet mine with an expression of apprehension. I stare at her knowing the last time I heard her voice was when I was on the phone with Adam in the lakes and she interrupted him, and surely this is what she is also remembering.

"Abigail," her tone is unsteady, she coughs clearing her throat before continuing. "I don't think I've got you down for a meeting today?" My eyes automatically roll thinking, is she serious. A meeting?

"That's because Kimberley, I haven't got one." A few people are sat waiting in the reception area, and although my back is to them, I can tell by Kimberly's face they're staring at me, because that was harsh how I answered.

"I can't let you go through; Mr Lord has a client with him." she stutters but my temper is somewhat fraying now.

"Really, that's good, because I need a witness." I reply sarcastically walking forward past the desk to make my way down the corridor.

"Abigail, you can't."

"I can't. Why? Will he shout at you again?" She stops herself from getting up and it's evident she's scared of him?

"He won't like it."

"Tough." I answer walking past her wondering what I'll do if she tries to stop me, but she doesn't. I feel scared myself knowing I had to work here, and this is where I met him. This is where I had to pretend, pretend that we had a happy marriage. That he never beat me. I had to lie to everyone and live my two lives, but it's not going to deter me this time. I walk past Bernard's office, then Jeff's, standing outside his. I can hear his slime of a voice inside and it's apparent to me that his client is a woman. She giggles at his comment, the line he uses to lure women. The line he used to lure me, and the rest of his victims, because victims we are, although some of us don't know it yet.

First the false sense of security - "You should think about what I said to you?" A pause from him to get their full attention, "if you like we can meet tomorrow?" then silence from him as she thinks about it, and as she thinks he goes for the kill. "Or, if you'd rather we can meet for a drink and make it less formal." Another pause while the bate is set.

"Yes, that would be better, I think." She replies, because he's convincing.

"You know it makes sense." He finishes.

"Oh, I do." And she takes the bate as if it was her idea. That's how he does it. As easy as that. Making you feel as though he's doing you a huge favour.

I blow out placing my hand on the door handle before turning it slowly to open, but it opens with a creak, which now alerts them someone is entering the room. His eyes fly to mine and are shocked that it's me standing there in his office, however, he tries to stay calm.

"Excuse me, we're in a meeting, close the door on your way out." She turns in my direction, and yes, she's young, pretty and well- groomed giving the appearance of money, and she looks totally naïve, just as I was, as where they all, but I can't let Adam lure her into his web of deceit. Words rush from my mouth,

"I'd leave and find another Solicitor, honestly you don't want this one." His stare is a warning, a grave warning of what is to come if I don't shut my mouth and leave. But I'm not leaving until I've made him pay and he gives me the signed divorce papers. She stands confused. Adam hands her his card as he's no choice he knows I'm not going to leave. "I'll be in touch." He says putting the card into her hand and lingering it there before pointing towards the door. And the poor girl walks towards me, her head down not speaking, and I wonder, no, pray that she's took heed. I move entering more into the office to let her pass and she doesn't make eye contact but leaves quietly. My heart is beating so fast I can literally hear it vibrating in my ears. His stare towards me is anger. But although I'm scared, I'm not backing down. He slams the door, but his voice doesn't raise. "What the fuck do you think you're playing at." I reach into my pocket taking out the pieces of paper and throw them up into the air, the yellow post-it-note is visible and lands on the carpet, message face up.

"No Adam, I want a divorce and you're going to sign those papers again." He laughs mockingly and starts walking towards me. I step back, aware of his temper and loose fists. He moves again, so, I step further back almost touching the wall. His head cocks to one side staring at my face, then his eyes move down my body. I swallow not knowing what he's doing because I wasn't expecting this reaction, he moves closer and I feel his breath on my face, it smells of Whiskey and mints, and I know he's trying to mask the fact that he's now drinking at work.

"Are those stocking you're wearing?" My face alters, he moves quickly towards the door, turns the key and locks it before throwing it across the room. My eyes dart in its direction. But he's back in front of me before I can move. He takes my face in his hand as I try to pull it away, but the more I pull the harder he squeezes my cheeks together. His face is almost touching mine, but then he licks his lips with his tongue before he runs it up the side of my face. My eyes close with dread and fear as I try my best to pull my knee up but my skirts to tight. Oh, God he's drunk. "Umm…" he slimes and does it again. I push him, but he pins me against the wall hard. I can't shout as his hand is still squeezing my mouth shut. I'm suddenly spun. I stumble, he pulls me back with my hair pushing me front first against the wall, my head hits it hard. My arms are grabbed quickly, and he pulls them behind me with strength.

"Get off me." I shout, but I'm stopped, as he squashes the side of my face against the wall.

He moves to my ear then whispers, "I'd shut the fuck up and listen if I were you, or I'll tie you, then gag you." Why didn't I listen to Edward, listen to my sub-conscious, why have I come here? Tears well my eyes, "Oh, dear, Abbie. Do you not like naughty Adam anymore." His voice is mocking, then nasty, "Turn around." I can't let him see me crying, that I'm scared. "I said turn the fuck around." He grabs my hair, turns me quickly then slams me back against the wall." His lip is out sulking. Then wham a slap to my face, his eyes raise at my reaction, my eyes are wide, and it hurts, then crack another. I scream hoping someone will hear me, but it's not audible, although it doesn't stop him from placing his hand to my mouth. I try to bite it, and he laughs, before, wham, another smack harder this time across my face and this sends me flying to the floor and he's on top of me in a split second, straddling me, his legs pinning my arms and I can't move, I try jolting and he smiles thrusting his hips forward towards my face.

"Umm...that's better I'm hard now, want to feel."

"No, let me go, just let me go." My voice is panicked and I'm losing control.

"Beg me too."

"Please, Adam just let me go." I try to push him but make no impression at all. "I'll scream."

"Then I'll ram my cock in your mouth." My eyes well with tears, tears I don't want him to see, but I'm scared, and he knows. "Are you scared, Abbie." His voice is quiet and calm.

"Please, I won't scream, just let me go, I'll not say anything." He smiles again and I'm so confused, because he appears mad. I've never seen him like this before he's always had a temper, a temper that I thought today I could use.

I'm panicking to get my breath, because I think he's flipped. His hand moves behind him, then quickly up my skirt. I gasp, but he covers my mouth, bile hits the back of my throat and I can't cough, I start to gag, I'm struggling to breathe. My eyes close as those dark memories are flooding my mind and I'm asking, 'please Lord help me, don't, don't let him do that,' but the images are strong and powerful and they don't want to leave my mind but I don't want to remember this….

I'm tied fast to a chair, gagged and naked, as he stands in front of me, his erection in his hand as he slowly masturbates, shouting,

"You disobedient hoar, this will teach you to go

behind my back, get another job, who do you think you fucking are?" Slap after slap then he removes the gag so he can hear me scream as he nips hard at my nipples and skin. My cries add to his excitement as tears stream my face and as the cries get louder the slaps come faster. I scream internally remembering the torcher, 'No, more' I'm back in the room, and he almost screeches at me but then stops as my tongue runs over the bridge in my mouth.

"Open your eyes I want to see the fear in them." I try hard to move, to fight, and fear is not the word I'd use as to what I'm thinking right now. But he removes his hand as quickly as he put it there. And I know he's fucking with my head. He reaches towards himself rubbing his erection. I sob knowing what he's going to do, he's going to rape me again. And I want to die.

I screw my eyes tighter shut not wanting to give him the satisfaction of see my fear, and he hits me repeatedly, because I won't open them and watch him getting off on hurting me. Then oddly my thoughts divert to Edward at what he's going to think, to say if he rapes me. I'm trying my best to distance myself from the situation, not to antagonise him any further because that is what he wants. He likes hurting me, seeing me scared, seeing the fear in my eyes, he rips at my blouse gaping it open,

"What's this piece of shit around your neck." He

taunts as though he's disgusted. My eye's fly open knowing he means the locket. He reaches for it. My eyes widen and I instinctively know I shouldn't have done that because he now knows it means something to me. "Oh, how sweet, is it for our babies, is it from Edward?" he turns it over then reads out loud, "aww... Abigail's two special angels," his voice suddenly changes to a rant, "but look" he rips it from my neck, then shoves it in front of my face, "No mention of Adam, the father." I think I'm going to stop breathing as he rams it back between my breast. His voice goes sulky, "Have we to keep it there next to your heart?" his expression is puzzled, "whoops, sorry." he snatches it again from my breast, "Oh, I almost forgot, you need to kiss it first don't you." He rams it to my lips, but all I can think of is how does he know that, how does he know I kiss it before I place it next to my heart, only Edward and I know that is what I do. His head cocks again with a puzzled expression and he looks truly deranged. "Penny not dropped yet?" I'm so confused, scared, terrified even at what he's going to do. His face is almost touching mine and I can see the aggression, it's as if he's Jekyll and Hide.

He hits the side of my head on the temple with a finger as though he's making a statement, "Reminder. Hair up in a clip, kiss the locket, place locket under black dress next to heart. I love you Edward Scott...."

I can't hear any more, my head is fussy, because he's just given me a blow by blow account of our night in London. How. How, does he know all this. His finger taps hard against the side of my head. "Got it yet. The fucking flowers they were from me." he almost sings in a mad voice. But I'd worked that out already. "God are you really that thick." He says, grinning as though he's won a competition. "Camera, Abbie, Camera." That word Camera haunts my mind. I'm trapped. We're trapped, because this is a pay-off and I've walked straight into it. What can I do, what does he want from me, from us? Suddenly there's a knock at the door.

"Mr Lord your 2 0 clock is here." It's Kimberley. His hand flies to my mouth but I know this is my chance. I try to shout but it's muffled. I bite again hard on his hand. He shouts,

"Bitch." But holds his hand firm on my mouth. I wriggle, push, kick, shout and bite again as hard as I can until I taste blood, but he still doesn't let go.

"Mr Lord, is everything, okay." She asks, before another knock. His eyes are telling me to stop, to keep still and stay quiet. But no, I won't. I push, I bite, I kick, then scream. She keeps knocking and then the door handle turns,

"Kimberley, what's the matter?" I hear a man's voice and I think it's Jeff. He glares then moves freeing me to sit forward.

"This is not the end." He darts towards the locket as I try to scramble too my feet to get it before him, but it's too late. Knocking and shouting continues from outside the door.

"Adam." Jeff shouts banging on the door, "open the door, what's going on." He doesn't answer. But he's trapped and can't get out. I scream,

"Jeff help, he's gone mad, and attack me." His face is rage, pure rage and this is the Adam I know. I stare at the locket. I can hear Jeff telling Kimberley to phone the police.

"Give me back the locket."

"Fuck off, this is a trade." He yells back almost frothing at the mouth,

"A trade for what." But I know exactly what, although I need him to say it.

"The pen-drive." I don't know how I manage to say my next words, but I do because I need to prove its him on the drive. I need witnesses to hear him say it.

"The pen-drive, where you're hurting and assaulting those women. Then give me back my locket." His temper is on full throttle as he looks for the key. I saw where it landed, but he didn't. He's panicking as he heard Kimberley was told to ring for the police. He's pacing around the office like a caged animal, then goes towards a safe at the back of the room, his back is to me, his breathing quick and he's losing his nerve fumbling with the code as his eyes scan the room for the key. I try to distract him, "Adam give me back the locket." Knocking continues, shouting and the handle keeps being turned, the door bangs, then bangs again, there trying to force their way in. His eyes move from the safe to the door and back again, suddenly it springs open but he's fast and bolts out of the room barging past Jeff who tries to grab him, but misses so he chases after him shouting,

"Adam what the hell is going on." I hear the door in the main reception open, people confused and talking,

"He ran out, I'm not sure I think up the high street towards the station." Then reality hits me as to what has just happened or what could have happened. I stumble, Kimberly steadies me with an arm guiding me to a seat. I stare at her, as she places her cardigan around my shoulders to cover my exposed body.

"Abigail, are you okay?" I stare, feeling numb. Lots of people have entered the office and start asking me questions. But I don't answer, I can't answer, I'm in shock knowing I've done this. I came here to get him to confess, sign the divorce papers, but he said nothing, instead I've made the situation a hundred times worse. He's hurt me again, stole the locket, filmed me and Edward at the hotel everything we did that night. It's bad and he'll use it now for sure. And Edward, God, knows what he's going to do.

"I think she's in shock, Jeff."

"Make her a cup of tea with plenty of sugar in." She goes to leave, but I grab her hand, knowing that she saved me from him. I shake my head as though I'm telling her not to go. She nod's and stays at my side.

"I'll stay with Abigail Jeff until the police arrive."

"As you wish."

I feel as though I'm going to pass out. Edward's going to be livid that I've come here, but he can't be as livid as I am at myself for coming here and making it worse. He told me over-and-over again not to do anything, but did I listen. No.

"Is there anyone I can ring for you?" My hand goes to my mouth, shaking as tears fill my eyes. "Hey, come on Abigail." But all I want is Edward, but I can't face him. I'm ashamed of what Adam has done to me, and what he could have done, that he filmed us. My hand goes to my heart, he's took my locket, my babies again from me and I want to curl into a ball, close my eyes and erase this day from my memory. Voices from outside fill the room,

"There in there, if you want to follow me. Abigail, the police are here and want to talk to you." I look up and see it's officer Johnson, she stares at me at first then realises who I am.

"Abigail, may I talk to you." I just stare back. Words

won't come.

"She's not spoken to anyone."

"As she asked for anyone." Johnson asks.

"No, she's in shock I think." She nods then leaves the room. I can hear her talking to Jeff but it's not registering what she's saying or what he's saying back.

Jeff returns and speaks quietly to Kimberley, "She's sent for someone else to come who she may speak too."

"Okay, I'll stay with her." But they could call anyone, the Pope even, but I don't think I could speak, I feel too ashamed. I can still hear lots of different voices outside the room. Kimberly starts telling me what's happening,

"They're taking statements from us and the clients that were in reception." But I don't acknowledge her. "Here Abigail let me take of your jacket and put my cardigan on you properly." I nod, as she takes my jacket, before pulling my arms through the sleeves of the cardigan. "See that's better isn't it?"

"Abigail, are you hurt, are you okay?" I shrug my shoulders looking up to see Simon. "Will you please talk to me." Tears well my eyes. He takes my hand. "Edwards on his way." I break down and cry scared to see him, because I know what his reaction is going to be. "Hey, what has happened." He asks staring at my face, probably the red marks that will no doubt bruise. His arm goes to go around me. I flinch and move, he appears shocked, "Why are you even here?"

I can't answer that question now, because I don't know why I'm here, or why I came, because this has turned so sour, and I certainly can't face Edward. The shouting, the broken promise I made, that I'd not do anything without telling him first. And him telling me, 'I told you not to do this.' I'm hurting badly not just physically but mentally and I'm not at all sure if he'll forgive me for this or if we can come back from it, and I'm also aware of how much I've hurt him by doing exactly what he told me not to do.

Chapter 22

My eyes close wishing I was anywhere else apart from here. The commotion that's now erupted in the reception area is loud, aggressive almost.

"Where is she Simon?"

"She's down there in the office, but you need to calm down first. She doesn't need this."

"Don't you tell me to calm down or tell me what to do." My eyes are still closed, knowing I've failed miserably, and that I don't want to face him, it's cowardly, I know that, but I'm scared, scared that he'll not see past why I came, why I tried to stop Adam - that I want a divorce so badly and him out of my life so that we can be together. More raised voices,

"Edward calm down." But he's not listening, as seconds later he bounds into the room, followed by Simon. I stand nervously, and with the look on his face it's evident he's more than annoyed. I pull at the cardigan wrapping it more around my shoulders but not before he sees my blouse is ripped, the red marks on my face and neck. And I can only imagine what's going through his mind, as it shows so much on his face. He takes a deep breath, as I walk towards him,

"I'm sorry." I manage, but he moves back away from me leaving me standing there frozen. I've lost him. My hand goes to my mouth, tears course my face as Kimberley places her arm around my shoulder and I stand and stare willing him to speak, to say something, anything, shout at me even, just to acknowledge I'm here. His eyes move from mine, his tone is enraged something I've never seen or heard before,

"Where the fuck is, he?" he blasts, addressing Simon.

"He's gone."

"Where?"

"We're not sure, towards the train station we think." He barges past Simon who makes a grab for his arm, I shout to him but it's as if we're both invisible. "Edward there's a warrant out for his arrest." but I'm not all together sure he heard him because he sprits through the door, followed by Simon almost chasing him, telling him to stop, "You'll make it twice as worse, Edward."

"Are you serious. I'm going to fucking kill him." The door to outside has opened just as I make it into the reception, but he doesn't look back he carries on through and out into the street followed by Simon hurtling after him. I almost fall to my knees as tears fall quickly, since I know this is all my fault. I should have listened. My thoughts were right, and he's not going to forgive me for this. I've lost his trust, because I've lied and broke my promise. I look at Kimberley, then glance the room, the police are taking statements from people as Johnson approaches,

"Abigail, I need you to come to the station with me."

"No. I want to go home."

"You can't Abigail, I need to get a statement from you."

"I said, I want to go home...please." I'm desperate to shower his dirty hands off my body. I want Edward to come home and forgive me. I want to start this day again. Kimberly breathes gently before speaking,

"Abigail, I think it's best you go with her and give a statement they need to know what he's done." And of course, I know she's right that I do need to do this, because I can't bury my head as I've done before, but I need to speak with Edward explain why I did, what I did. I can't seem to think straight. All I can see are his eyes, that at first, I thought looked blank, but they weren't blank, they were disappointed and hurt. Johnsons phone rings, she answers moving slightly away.

"Sir...Yes, I'll speak to her and explain."

"Abigail, Simon has said I need to escort you to the hospital first to get you checked over, before I take you to the police station to make a statement. Is that alright with you?" I somehow get a glimmer of hope from this, thinking, this could be Edwards suggestion. So, I agree and follow her out to the car that's parked on the main road in full view of everyone watching the commotion, although again I don't pay much attention to peoples remarks or comments on what is going on. I just robotically open the door to the back and sit waiting for her to get in staring blankly into space out of the window trying to ignore the pointing and elbowing from on lookers outside to get a better view of me as I suspect their wondering what's happening.

The drive to the hospital is silent, and we finally arrive at A & E, St Mary's which is relatively quiet. As we approach the desk quite a few people stare in my direction nudging each other as if to say, look at her, but there again I am being escorted by the police. Johnson appears to know the drill, as she asks,

"If you'll take a seat Abigail and let me book you in it will be quicker." So, I perch on the end of a seat with my back to everyone else who is waiting just so that I don't have to make eye contact with them and to avoid a conversation. But I'm aware all eyes are on me. She talks to the receptionist and points in my direction, then she calls me over. "Thank you." She says, "We can go around to room 2 the Doctor will see you." I nod, following behind as she seems to know where she's going making me wonder how many time's she's done this.

We enter the room and I'm hoping it's nobody who knows me, and to my relief it's not.

"Hi Abigail, I've a brief report of what's happened." Remarks the young female doctor moving some papers around on her desk. "Please, take a seat." Her smile appears kind as I sit on the chair opposite to her. "I need to ask you some awkward questions, are you alright answering for me. Do you want the officer to stay?" I shrug. "Did he rape you?" My head shakes. "Touch you intimately?" At first, I'm taken aback at the sensitivity of the question and bluntness by means of getting to the point. But there again I suppose she must ask and there's no point pussy footing around.

"No. No, nothing like that."

"Good." And she genuinely means it. "Okay let's look at your face." She stands, smiling kindly towards me as her hands place on my skin making me flinch. "Your head has it been banged?" I nod. "I think I'd like to send you for an X-Ray just because of the bruising and swelling that's appearing. I also need to ask you some questions first. "Is there any possibility you could be pregnant?"

"No."

"You're using precautions?"

"Yes."

"Birth control?"

"Yes,"

"Which one?"

"Cilest." She nods and writes it down.

"Are you in a relationship?"

"Yes."

"When was your last period?"

"Last month."

"When last month?" I shrug rolling my eyes as I know I'm bad at keeping records like that. "Was it normal?"

"I think so." She continues to write my answers down, then smiles.

"Abigail, just to be on the safe side as you're not one-hundred-per-cent sure about dates as a precaution would you consider having a pregnancy test as an X-Ray could be very harmful to the foetus if you were to be pregnant."

"Yes, then of course I'll do one, but I think it's a waste of time." She nods handing me a small paper bowl. "Go to the toilet and wee in that then hand it to the nurse." I leave the room and head for the toilet, do the sample, hand it to the nurse as asked, before returning to the room. They're talking when I enter but soon stop when they see me. Johnson quickly changes the subject,

"Abigail, can I get you a cup of tea or coffee?" The doctor looks up.

"You can stay here it shouldn't take long. I've asked the nurse to test it and it will give an immediate answer, should only take 10 minutes or so. I'll do your blood pressure and ob's while we wait." She seems nice and calm as she takes my observations then writes them down on a chart as I now sit in silence wondering about Edward.

Johnson has said nothing although I'm sure she's in contact with Simon. I've no bag or phone with me as they are back in the office at the deli which makes me think off gran, it's sort of slipped my mind with everything that's happening. She'll be worried to death. Johnson returns.

"Please may I use your phone." She nods handing it to me. The doctor looks up, "I'll see if your results are ready." A discrete way I think of leaving me to make the call, she eye's Johnson to follow her. I blow out, God what am I going to say. I ring her number. she answers almost immediately.

"Hello it's me."

"Where are you?"

"I'm at the hospital."

"What"

"Don't worry nothing serious, I twisted my ankle, and an old lady insisted on taking me to get it checked out." Silence and I know I'm not believed but honestly, I panicked and that was the first thing that came into my head.

"Really, Abigail."

"Umm…" I reply closing my eyes knowing I hate lying to her.

"Your mobile is here on the desk in the office and has been constantly ringing. Edward each time."

I rub my head with my hand, I'm not sure why, maybe to give me some time to answer or for inspiration, because I wonder if he wants to talk or shout at me. "I'll have to go now they are calling me for the X-Ray on my ankle." Another lie.

"So, you really are at the hospital?"

"Yes."

"Which, one." My eyes close because this is getting deeper, so do I lie about that as well?

"St Mary's, look, please can I explain when I get home."

"Okay." she hangs up and she also sounds disappointed with me as she knew I was telling lies and hiding something. I quickly dial Edwards number, it rings, and rings then goes to voice mail.

"Scott - leave a message."

"It's me. I've no phone it's at the office. Ring Johnsons phone please if you're still speaking to me. And I'm so sorry Edward, I truly am." I inhale, as tears start that I can't stop, knowing I've lied to gran, to Edward, broke my promise again. and truthfully, I'm scared, and I need a hug, and it's evident that I'm crying leaving the message as I hang up.

Simon, said to Edward, that they'd put a warrant out for Adam's arrest and I'm wondering if they've caught him, although I'm sure Johnson would have said something. I just hope Simon has managed to talk some sense into Edward and stopped him from looking, but there again did I listen. No, I didn't, but I wish to God I had, because I wouldn't be in this mess now. I'm just hoping that he'll forgive me for what I've done, although I can't blame him if he doesn't or doesn't trust me anymore. I sit waiting and it feels like hours, but it's only been five minutes. Johnson enters back with a tea.

"Thank you." I say, taking a sip, before she stands to the side on guard of the door. There's a knock and Doctor Russ enters holding a piece of paper. She nods towards me then at Johnson before asking her to step outside while she speaks to me. I hand Johnson her phone as she leaves.

"I have your results." My eyes don't leave hers because I think I know what she's going to say.

"It's positive."

"Are you sure?"

"There ninety-eight percent accurate."

"But I've had periods and use birth control?"

"Have you been sick or ill?"

"I was yesterday, but I can't remember now." A flush of panic hit's me as It dawns on me, my baby. My hand goes to my tummy holding it their knowing what Adam did to me, by slamming me against the wall, hitting me, knocking me to the floor. And despite everything that has happened or is about to happen my focus is on my baby now and nothing else matters.

"My baby is it going to be alright?"

"You've had no bleeding?"

"No." She can see the panic in my eyes, my hands shaking, "It has to be alright I can't lose another baby."

"You've been pregnant before?"

"Yes, twice." Her tone is sympathetic.

"And lost them both." My lip quivers as I try to hold back tears.

"We need to take some blood from you, Abigail."

"Why, what's wrong?"

"Nothing, it's routine it's called an HCG it's a hormone test to see if everything is well and how far gone you are."

"And how long is that going to take?"

"The results take about four to five hours."

"God, this is cruel you can't keep me waiting that long. Please, please Doctor Russ don't make me wait that long." My hands won't stop shaking, my legs are dancing. She moves raising from her seat and walks towards the door opening it.

"Officer Johnson, please could you escort Abigail to the Ultra-sound suite."

"Thank you, thank you, so much." I answer gratefully as my tears now stream my cheeks.

"I'll ring through and tell them to expect you." Tears continue to fall as I leave and follow Johnson down the corridors to the entrance of the scan rooms.

"Are you okay, Abigail?" I shake my head petrified, scared and feeling sick. She doesn't say anything else but it's obvious she knows. Johnson walks to the desk and in a low voice gives my name. The reception lady nods.

"Yes, go through their expecting her." I follow behind Johnson, a nurse comes out of a side room,

"Hi, is it Abigail." I nod. "Would you like to follow me." We enter the room and Johnson stays outside. "If you'd just like to pop up onto the bed for me." I do as I'm asked almost mechanically. "Just a few questions first." She say's and I answer them desperate for her to start, because all I want to know is my baby okay. I remember these rooms, the sad news these rooms brought me. And now I just need to know. "If you'd like to lie down" then she starts explaining what is going to happen, but I'm not listening although I'm nodding my head in agreement. The jelly is place on to my tummy and I remember the coldness of it on my skin, she then places the hand-held scanner on top and starts to circle it around looking at the monitor which is out of my view. She moves it around my tummy spreading the cold gel underneath. It's a familiar feeling, and not a pleasant one. My mind is all over the place and I want to take it from her and shout, just tell me what you see but it feels like hours not seconds and it's unbearable. I can't take it anymore and splutter through tears,

"Please, please, tell me is everything alright…please, speak to me and tell me." Because this is what they did before, turned the monitor away from me so I couldn't see and I'm praying and bargaining with God, to let my baby be okay. I've no thoughts of anything else as I hold my breath waiting for this woman to speak. This woman with my fate. my hope, my dreams in her hands.

She smiles kindly before turning the monitor towards me. My heart nearly jumps from my chest not knowing the outcome, then there's shouting outside from the corridor, her eyes lift, my head shakes for her to ignore it and continue because I need to know, and I need to know now. I almost shout this time,

"Please, just tell me." The screen looks fuzzy and I can't see anything. My hand flies to my mouth and a loud whimper escapes, I can't see anything, there's nothing there, only white streams of dust on a black background like a falling snow drift running down the monitor screen. White noise I think they call it, but this has no sound and no noise, the only noise I can hear is internally and that is screaming in my head.

"It's okay, see, see that," she points, "That flash." I nod. "That's your babies' heart-beat." A very strange noise now erupts from my lips and the tears fall faster,

"Mine! My babies, heart-beat."

"Yes, and it appears normal and healthy." The shouting's got louder outside the room, and It's Edward who is doing the shouting, but his voice is panicked.

"Sir, I said you can't come down here."

"Johnson, where is she, what's wrong, why are they doing an ultra-sound nobody will tell me anything?"

"Sir, I said…"

"I heard what you said. Do you know who I am?"

"I think I've seen you around sir, but that will not stop me calling security if you don't stop shouting, Mr Scott." I hear Edward huff at her response,

"Call who the hell you like, because I'm not leaving."

"Mr Scott please calm down." Johnson follows trying her best to defuse the whole situation.

"Which room is she in Johnson." He demands pacing outside. I think the woman's left and more so it's apparent that she's gone for security. "Answer me." He blasts, but Johnson's holding her ground.

"They won't let you in unless Abigail says it okay."

"I fucking know that." My eyes raise through tears, as

does the nurses. He's really annoyed because he'd never swear like that.

"Do you know him then?" the nurse asks, a little tongue-in-cheek as I'm sure she also knows who he is. I nod staring towards the closed door with my mouth practically open. "Do you want him to come in?"

"Yes, but please don't tell him about the baby." I ask her, knowing that I need to know if he's forgiven me and he's not just going to forgive me, because I'm pregnant with his child.

"That's not my place to tell him or say anything, that is up to you to do so, would you like five minutes alone?"

"Please."

"Then I'll open the door and let him in before Joy has him arrested, because I don't think he's going to calm down until he's seen you, do you?" She opens the door and calls his name, he answers firmly but before she can continue, he's in the room. His stride to the bed is long before grabbing hold of me tightly, whispering,

"I'm so sorry I left you, but I had too. Are you okay?" he looks at me with panic, gliding his hand down the side of my face making me flinch, his lip pulls in, his eyes close but he contains his temper, instead calmly asking the nurse,

"Why are you doing an Ultra-sound, what's wrong?" His voice sound scared, and I think I know what he's thinking, but I also know he's forgiven me. "Are you hurting inside."

"No. No, I'm not. I've a few bruises as you can see but they'll go, and I've also a few apologies to make, but more so I've something to show you." He looks puzzled as I nod to the nurse, and she places the scanner back onto my tummy. "look at the monitor." He does and looks confused. I so want to tell him, but I want to see his face, I want to let him see the flutter for himself and hopefully he'll feel the same as I do.

The screens fuzzy, his head moves towards it, his eyes squint trying to focus on the white snow as I point to the quickening flash, and he knows, of course he knows, and although his face appears fixed in a state of shock, his body language tells me he knows. But now I'm uncertain of his thoughts because he's not giving much away, he stares almost in disbelief his eyes darting from the monitor to mine. As though he's processing it or deliberating on what to say. The screen freezes as the nurse removes the scanner, "I'll leave you two alone." She whispers walking from the room.

"Abbie," he speaks my name and it seems to linger in the room as I wait for another, but it doesn't come and I'm still uncertain and now scared that he doesn't want the baby. His expression remains frozen, but I know if I must do this alone, then I will. His head shakes as though he's dumbstruck but then just as I'm sitting wondering what to do his smile comes, his hand places gently on my tummy, his eyes meet mine, and they looked glazed and his voice is a croak as he speaks, "My baby? Our, baby?" My eyes screw tight, but it doesn't stop the tears. "Hey, hey, don't cry," his voice is wobbly as he wipes the tears from my cheek, his arms gently envelope me, a tender sweet kiss he places on my lips, whispering, "You, clever girl." He breathes in so deep and it sounds content, pleased and relieved all at the same time. He lifts my chin to look into my eyes, and his are smiling back at me, and my smile is far too wide to be measured, because this is love. Love that we are both feeling.

And love in its purest form.

Printed in Poland
by Amazon Fulfillment
Poland Sp. z o.o., Wrocław